Homer, a bluetick hound pup Compton's heart. It is the early 1970s, and the dog, ears, mottled fur, and appetite, gives Jeb a reason to get up in the morning after his wife, Annie, passes on. Another reason is the town's newspaper, the *Hurlin Express*, which he reads religiously, usually sitting on his front porch in Arkansas, where he can hear his soybean crops rustle in the wind. Within its pages, he finds stories of his neighbors, mostly salt-of-the-earth people struggling with the toils of everyday life.

Even if you've never stepped foot in the South, you'll feel as if you're walking beside Jeb and Homer, smelling the dewy grass, and hearing the twang of a perfect southern voice. You'll step into a debate club where Bart Scoggins, the elementary football coach, tries to convince the crowd that one of their own has fallen victim to the mad handiwork of space aliens.

You'll meet John Winston and the fainting goats he raises, but has to sell to keep his wife happy. And witness two grown men fighting for the hand of a lady – by playing a game of pool.

You'll go to work with Bertie May Johnson, pie champion, who loves to eat the way other people love breathing. She's about fed up with her job as a taste-tester who's not allowed to swallow the food she's given.

Before the book ends, you'll feel as if you've spent a year in Hurlin, the town still talking about their snake handling preacher who set the congregation scrambling after a mishap of Biblical proportions; the out-of-town antique dealer who discovers the real worth of a family heirloom; and, of course, the salvation of Jeb Compton because of a little girl and a hound who seems to hold the wisdom of the ages inside his old hard head.

# HOME IS

*Where The*

# HOUND IS

BY BILL WILWERS

Book cover model: Heidi
Heidi's parents: Barry and Sarah Bartholomew
Book cover photographer: Kim Bice

# CHAPTER 1 — THE ROAD TO HURLIN

Jeb and Annie Compton sat on their porch in the matching white oak rockers he had fashioned years ago. In the still of this early evening, whippoorwills recited their litanies while Spot-winged Glider dragonflies wheeled and banked to decimate the ranks of mosquitoes and gnats. A light breeze, unusual for that time of year, rustled the leaves of the big sycamore tree in the yard and eased the effects of the sweltering Arkansas heat and humidity. Their daily tasks behind them, the couple quieted for a bit — Jeb with the hometown newspaper, the *Hurlin Express*, and Annie mending a tear in a pair of his overalls.

Annie, petite and frail of constitution, but possessing a steely core of fierce determination, looked fondly at her husband. "Hey, Jeb, how do you manage to get so many blamed holes in your clothes? It's not like the soybeans give you that much of a struggle."

Jeb, six-feet tall and sturdy, with unruly brown hair that defied his attempts to tame it, looked over. At fifty-one years old, he could still outwork a man half his age and took pride in knowing that he could.

"I don't know, Annie. They can get pretty testy when they think I ain't tending them proper."

Annie snorted and went back to her mending. After a bit, she stopped. "Hey, Jeb, is there anything in that paper I should know about?"

This was a common question for Annie to ask. A new decade had recently rolled in, and now they were living in the 1970s, although time nearly stood still in their little part of the world. Still, if there was anything Annie needed to know, it was likely in the newspaper.

Jeb considered. "Well, it's hard to say. Lem Johnson's got some tarps for sale."

"Do we need any tarps?"

"Nope."

"Well, what else?"

Jeb considered again. "Seems the mayor is running for re-election. He got a rally planned down on the square."

"Does he have an opponent?"

"Nope, but he's going ahead with it anyway."

Annie shook her head. "Any excuse for that man to blow and go."

"Yep."

"What else?"

Jeb laid the copy of the *Hurlin Express* in his lap. "You wanting to read this by any chance?"

Annie smiled. "Nope. Hey, Jeb?"

Jeb smacked his head with an open hand. "Woman, are you trying to drive me balmy?"

Annie looked contrite. "No, I ain't. I'm just feeling a tad

melancholy, and I hoped I could get you to tell me your story."

Jeb feigned exasperation, although truth be told, he'd stand on his head if it meant lifting Annie's spirits. "Ain't you tired of hearing that, woman? I told it to you not a month ago."

Annie frowned. "Not one bit tired of hearing it, Jeb. It's important to me. I like hearing where you came from and what led you here. Besides, each time you tell it, it's a bit different."

Jeb blew out a breath and set the paper down on the porch. He looked at his wife. Her long hair had thinned, and gray fought a winning battle with auburn for dominance, but she was still a beauty. "It do cover quite a span, though. With your kind permission, ma'am, I'll be hopping around some and doing some picking and choosing."

Annie shot him a glare, but her eyes laughed. "Do it as you see fit, but put a lid on those sassy remarks."

Jeb shut his eyes for a second, calling up those old memories. "Yes, ma'am," he said. "Well, let's see, my sister Ellie and me was brought up in California."

Annie nodded. "But you weren't born there."

Jeb lowered his eyebrows. "Who's telling this tale? No, I were born in Oklahoma. Pa were born in California, though, and they hauled me with them looking for work. It went good for a piece, till the Depression caught up to us. After that, the sawmills shut down, and we had to work them pea fields for next to nothing. Pa got sick and died, and we barely scraped by. Mama was already carrying Ellie by then, and she were born on the road, never knowing our pa. If a feller named Sam hadn't crossed our path, I don't know if we'd a made it."

"Tell me more about Sam," Annie said.

"Nicest man you ever did see. He was white headed by the

7

time we met him. Down on his luck for a few years by then, I suspect. I say that because he knowed how to get by on almost nothing. We was working the fields with him one day when Mama near about broke apart. She doubled over, her tears dropping onto the ground in front of her. That night, Sam came by our ragged tent, brought us a silver dollar, a fortune to us back then, and offered to look out for us. He bedded down in front of the tent every night after that, and us kids stumbled over him more than once when we had to answer the call of nature. Every Friday, when the boss man paid us, he'd give half his take to Mama. Claimed it was for rent. Imagine that, paying rent for sleeping in front of our tent."

Jeb grew silent and looked down at the oak planks on the porch. After a minute, he looked up. "Them was hard times. If you don't mind, Sugar Pie, I'll save the details for another day."

Annie's soft brown eyes welled up. She reached over and put her hand over his much larger one. "That's fine."

Jeb cleared his throat. "Anyways, things went on like that for a few more years. By the end of the 1930s, the Depression finally wore itself down. Ma had had her fill of California, and she hankered to move back to Oklahoma. Sam decided to come with us, and that old Pontiac had just enough left in her to get us there. We stayed with relatives for a piece till Sam found work in the oil fields. By then, we thought of him like family."

Jeb stood, stretched, and looked down at Annie. He loved these summer nights when the sky stayed light till nearly bedtime. "That be good enough for you?"

Annie stopped sewing. "You know danged well you're not finished. Hey, where are you off to?"

Jeb paused halfway to the front door and turned around.

8

He cast his eyes heavenward as if seeking deliverance. "I thought you might say that, but I'm getting powerful parched from all this talking. I were just going to get some lemonade to wet my whistle. Do you want some?"

Annie tried to hide a smile. "I suppose, but don't you forget to get back out here. And mind you don't sugar it up too much."

"I hear you, woman." Jeb returned to the porch with two filled mason jars, one with extra sugar. He kept that one and handed the other to Annie. He looked toward the soybean field. He couldn't see the three-foot-high plants, but he could just barely hear them swaying in the breeze that skittered across the land.

Plopping back down in his chair, he took a big gulp of his lemonade and continued. "Them oil fields didn't call to me, and I were itching to strike out on my own," Jeb said. "World War II were ramping up, and I signed up in the army. Eighteen years old, but I already felt like a old man. Got stationed at Fort Chaffee up by Fort Smith. Just a hundred and fifty miles from where we sit here in Hurlin, Annie, but it seemed as far away as California. Anyway, I got sent overseas right quick and saw some fighting."

Jeb grew silent again. Annie glanced over at him but didn't speak. She understood he didn't like to talk about that time, and she never pressed him. She knew that over thirty-five hundred Arkansas boys never saw home again, and she thanked God that he'd made it out alive. After a few minutes, Jeb gave his head a shake and resumed speaking.

"After the war, I had me some money saved up, and I looked around for something to do with myself. A fella in my unit come from Hurlin, right here in Garland County, and he always talked about how he missed it. Told me land were cheap, farming were good, and folks was friendly. Seemed like I were always hungry growing up, and the thought of a steady supply of food were kind of appealing, so I thumbed a ride down here to have a look-see. Ended up buying this here forty acres with this small house, barn, and stock pond, and I learned how to farm. There were some rough patches and plenty of ignorance to overcome, but I were used to that."

Annie chuckled, then grew quiet. "Hey, Jeb?"

Jeb looked at her.

"Let's skip to the part about how you met me."

Jeb raised his eyebrows. "What be the hurry all of a sudden?"

Annie looked down at Jeb's tattered overalls in her lap. She ran her fingers back-and-forth over the coarse denim. "Well, if you don't know already, it's my favorite part."

Jeb smiled. "Okay, then. After a few years, I were making some headway, but it seemed like there were something missing. I'd made me some friends around town, and had me some good neighbors, but it were still kind of lonely somehow. Then one day, me and Joe Hicks piled in his old Chevy and took off to Hot Springs to see the sights. We was strolling down West Grand Avenue when I seen a vision walk toward me. She were the prettiest gal I ever did see, and she near about stopped my heart."

Even though Annie suspicioned what was coming, she played along. "Was it me?"

Jeb grinned. "Nope, but when she took a few more steps, I could see you staring in front of a shop window."

Annie reached over and whacked him on the arm. "You're terrible. Now tell it like it really was."

Jeb held up his hands as if fending off a threat. "Yes, ma'am. Well, I turned to tell Joe I were going over to talk to you, but he were nowhere in sight. Maybe he took off after that first gal we seen and didn't bother to tell me. Didn't change my intention, none.

"Now, Annie, here's the truth. That other gal weren't half the looker you was. Seeing you were like looking at a vision. I pinched myself to make sure I weren't dreaming. Then I come over to you, but you didn't notice. Your eyes was glued to that dress in the store window. I got your attention, introduced myself, and I for sure won you over right then and there with my sweet talk."

Annie smiled. "That's how you remember it, is it? I seem to recall things a bit different."

"Do tell."

"I remember looking at the dress. It had a navy-blue pleated skirt, and I was working out how it was made, figuring I could make one just like if I could find the right material. I looked away for a moment and noticed this tall fellow standing beside me. All gangly and gawky, he could barely string three words together and didn't seem to know what to do with his hands. They fluttered all around him like the wings of a mockingbird."

Jeb raised his eyebrows. "You must have got me confused with some other fella."

"Nope, it was you all right."

Jeb scratched his head. "Huh. Well, however it went, we hit it off, and before too long we was keeping company."

He grinned. "Anyways, I think you can take the rest of the story from there."

Annie reached for Jeb's hand and gave it a squeeze. "Yes."

# CHAPTER 2 — ARRIVAL AND DEPARTURE

Jeb Compton reckoned that O'Neill fella probably had the right of it. He didn't recollect exactly how the writer's quote went, but he recalled the first line well enough: "None of us can help the things life has done to us." The rest talked about how each thing life throws at a man changes him, pushing him toward something else entirely, until he ends up losing who he used to be. When cancer took Jeb's wife, he looked in her gilded mirror that hung above the fireplace and saw a stranger.

Over the next dark months, despite the attempts of old friends and the tasks he set himself to keep going, only one thing kept him hanging on. "Hey, Homer, come here, boy." This was addressed to a young, forty-pound bluetick coonhound. Homer sat in a bare, sunny patch in the front yard, idly scratching his side with his back paw. When the dog heard his name, Homer raised up off his rear, ambled over to the porch steps where Jeb sat, and laid his head on Jeb's knee.

"You know, Homer, losing Annie tore me up considerable. But I'm trying to keep on a plugging. Plus, I got you to worry about." Homer cocked what passed for his eyebrow. He seemed to be asking if maybe Jeb didn't have that sentiment turned around.

Annie had given Homer to Jeb on the last Christmas they spent together, and the hound was doubly dear to him because of that. Of course, Annie had included a little poke to go with it: "If you're going to keep traipsing all over those woods after possums and coons, I 'spect you'd best have something to give you half a chance at finding them."

Eighteen months before, Annie, wrapped in her nightdress and robe, sat in the white oak rocker Jeb had made for her so long ago. The embers in the fieldstone fireplace kept her warm enough, she reckoned, but that last chemo session had worn on her something fierce, and she shivered anyway. She'd feel poorly for the next few days, and then, when it finally lightened up, it would be time for the next go-round. The worst thing about it, though, was knowing that it didn't matter. Her time on Earth was nearly up, and she could sense that there was nothing anyone could do to change that. In fact she knew it. Doc Wilkens knew it. She thought Jeb knew it too, though he would never admit it.

Annie gazed at her husband, who was sitting beside her. It had been quite a ride these past twenty-four years, she thought, and it had been good for most of them. Her only regrets were not being able to have younguns and her knowing that she'd soon have to leave Jeb to fend for himself. Maybe this one last surprise could help with that. With some effort, she lifted her right arm and pointed to the sparsely decorated spruce tree that had come from the grove behind their house. "Go ahead and get your present," Annie said to Jeb.

Jeb got the large box, carried it back to his sturdy oak chair with the threadbare cushion, sat down, and opened it. He pulled out a wriggling ball of coarse, shiny fur, its colors so mixed together the pup resembled a well-used artist's palette. Its muzzle was tan, as were the large dots just above its soulful brown eyes.

Before he could examine the pup any further, Annie said, "I just knew you'd love him!"

So, the pup's a male, Jeb thought, and he felt a surge of pride as he continued examining the dog. Its head and ears, which dangled down like hand towels, were colored mostly black, but a goodly chunk of white trickled down from his brow to his bulb-like nose and draped off to the sides. His body was off-white with a speckled pattern that reminded Jeb of some thrush eggs he'd seen. Several large black spots decorated his sides, rump, and part of his front legs, with the rest being tan and white.

"Is it me, or do he have a blue shade to him?" Jeb asked.

"The breeder told me that comes from those black specks on the white coat. He called it 'ticking' and said that's where the bluetick gets its name."

"Huh. Well, he be a peculiar sight, no doubt, but —" Jeb's hesitation didn't have anything to do with the pup. But at that moment he was wondering if he'd have time to train the little rascal. Lately, his days were spent working the farm and taking care of Annie.

The thought made his eyes well. "Thank you, dear. I love the little fella."

Annie smiled. "You're welcome, but I don't imagine he'll be little for none too long. Did you notice the size of his paws? That breeder said he could grow to eighty pounds and be up to two feet high at the shoulder." Her smile widened. "He also said that breed could really be a handful."

Jeb looked down at the pup who was busily worrying the sleeve of Jeb's flannel shirt and giving off small, fierce-sounding growls. "How did you manage all this, Annie? I've been with you every waking second this last month, far as I know."

Annie flat-out loved surprises. "Fayette and Demus helped me. Even brought the little guy here this morning when I sent you to the store for pickles." Annie laughed. "We didn't need pickles on Christmas Eve."

Fayette and Demus lived down the road, as fine a couple as Jeb had ever met. Well, he thought, he'd be sure to thank them next time their paths crossed.

"You amaze me, Annie Compton. After all that trouble, let's give him a fitting name he can grow into."

He thought on it a minute. "I always liked reading that Greek fella's stories. You know, the ones about them Greeks and Trojans feuding."

Annie nodded. "*The Odyssey*," she said. "I right liked that myself. Never made it through *The Iliad*."

Jeb hoisted up the pup and looked him in the eyes. "What do you say to Homer, best poet in all of ancient Greece?"

The pup blinked once and wrinkled up his face as though considering the matter. Then he licked Jeb's nose.

"Homer it be then."

Homer grew like the proverbial weed and shared many of the same traits: he was stubborn, aggravating, and always popping up where he wasn't wanted. Whether messing around in the garbage pail, digging after a gopher in Annie's garden that Jeb was now tending, sprawled out on Jeb's pillow, or lying where Jeb could trip over him, Homer found a way to keep things stirred up. He also had a distinct musky odor that sometimes had Jeb checking to see if his deodorant had quit on him.

On the plus side, Homer was devoted, smart, and protective, and he had a real knack for treeing critters once he'd caught their scent. With Homer being naturally inclined to follow any interesting smell, Jeb had a chore training him. On their daily walks, Jeb kept Homer on a tight leash. Only when he was ready to come when hollered for, did Jeb let him loose on his own.

The hound needed room to roam, and Homer likely covered every square inch of Jeb's forty acres on a daily basis. The squirrels in the hickory grove got his special attention, and they returned it by pelting him with nuts and chattering a good what-for. Mockingbirds and jays, a quarrelsome lot in their own right, got fired up when Homer came calling. You could hear his bawling howl a far piece, and on more than one occasion, Jeb jerked upright from a nap as Homer caught a fresh scent and took off.

Annie doted on the hound and spoiled him rotten. Whenever Jeb looked for him after some incident involving mischief, he first checked with Annie. Chances were good that Homer would be hiding behind her chair, where she sat more and more near the warmth of the fireplace. Before Jeb could launch into his grievance, Annie would hold up a restraining hand before lowering it to pat the large head that suddenly found its way onto her lap.

"Now, Jeb, leave him be. Whatever he did, he didn't mean any harm. He's still a rambunctious pup, and he's going to test you some."

Jeb would always relent. Annie looked frailer with each passing day, and there was no way he would upset her. If she insisted on vouching for that aggravating hound, he thought, then he would let it slide.

The days passed, and Annie grew weaker. Homer stayed by her side to offer what comfort he could, and Jeb gave her his every spare moment and then some. He helped get her ready in the morning and brushed her thinning hair. He made her meals and tried to coax her dwindling appetite. He held her hair back when her stomach rebelled and emptied its contents. He read to her from her favorite books and played the old gospel records that she loved on the phonograph. He reminisced about their years together and tried to draw out a smile by telling her about Homer's latest misdeeds. And always, Jeb struggled to hold back his tears.

One cold January evening, after an especially bad day, Annie looked up at him as she lay on the sofa. In a weak voice, she said, "You know, Jeb, I don't think it will be long now."

Jeb looked stricken. "What are you saying, Annie? I know today were not a good one for you, but —"

Annie stopped his protest with a gentle touch on his arm. "It's all right, Jeb. I love you. You and Homer look out for each other, and I'll be waiting to see you on the other side." She smiled and closed her eyes.

Jeb couldn't think what to do. He could call the 911 service that had recently made its way to Hurlin, but it would take at least thirty minutes for an ambulance to arrive this far out in the country. He could carry Annie to his truck, but the ride to the hospital on the bumpy roads might do her in. Still, he had to try. He stood up, grabbed his truck keys from the top of his dresser, and came back.

When he looked at his hands, they were shaking.

He kissed Annie's forehead and said, "I'm gonna get you to the hospital, Annie. They'll know what to do." He was crying by then, and tears fell onto Annie's face. He shook her arm gently, and she didn't respond, so he lowered his ear to her chest and listened. Her heart made no sound. He checked her pulse. Nothing.

Jeb and Homer — the dog hadn't left her side — stared at each other for a moment, then both threw back their heads and shared a mournful howl.

Neither Jeb nor Homer slept that night. Jeb wandered the house, picking up photos of Annie, touching the costume jewelry she kept in a Whitman's chocolates box in their closet, running his fingers across the clothes that hung lifeless on padded hangers. Homer walked every step with Jeb, bumping into his master every time Jeb stopped.

After the funeral, Jeb returned to the empty house and untied Homer from the sycamore tree in the front yard. He'd been afraid to leave him loose, knowing the dog would follow his truck to town. He looked at his hound through red-rimmed eyes and bent down to hug his neck. "It were a nice service, Homer. Lots of well-wishers and flowers. Annie were loved by many a folk. I'm sorry I couldn't take you with, but we will go visit her soon."

He buried his face in Homer's coarse fur. "It's hard, Homer. Harder than anything I can think of. I'm going to be needing your help to get through this."

Homer pulled back, licked Jeb's face, and barked once — a sad bark, but a determined one.

# CHAPTER 3 — COMMON GROUND

As he sipped a cup of Earl Grey tea, Hector Deakins eyed the newspapers arrayed on his round oak kitchen table. He subscribed to all the editions from the surrounding Arkansas towns, and he began his workday by checking in each.

"Let's try this one, shall we, Max?" he said as he picked up a copy of the *Hurlin Express*.

The recipient of his comment, a sleek Siamese cat, lay curled on the table in a pool of sunlight. Max opened one eye, gave a dismissive sniff, and went back to sleep.

Hector opened the paper to the classified ad section. He didn't expect to find much of interest, but one never knew. The usual assortment of used cars, tractors, and furniture appeared as he scanned the columns. His eyes stopped on one ad.

FOR SALE — Ornately carved, 3-foot, gold-gilded mirror. Excellent condition, circa 1920. Will sell for $20.00 or best offer. Call 831-7448.

"How intriguing, Max. This ad piques my interest. First is the wording: o*rnately* and *circa*. You don't often encounter such a vocabulary in these smaller towns. And the description of the mirror. It sounds like an antique, which could make it worth much more than the asking price. If so, why would the owner sell it so cheaply? In fact, why is the owner selling it at all? And what about its history? How did the owner obtain it? So many interesting questions. I think this is certainly worth checking out, don't you?"

Max apparently did not. He uncurled, stretched, yawned, and hopped off the table to seek a resting place unbothered by conversation. Hector got up, went over to the wall-mounted phone, dialed the number, and waited. The call was answered on the fourth ring.

"Morning."

"Good morning, sir. I'm Hector Deakins, and I'm calling about your ad in the paper — the one for the mirror. To whom am I speaking?"

"I'm Jeb Compton. So, you is interested in that mirror?"

"Yes, indeed. I would very much like to see it."

"Well, sir, if you can swing by the house, you can have a look-see for your own self."

"I can certainly do that. If you'll give me directions from downtown Hurlin — I know the route that far — and a good time to come by, I'll do that very thing."

"Good enough. I'm usually working them soybeans pretty early and don't finish up till four or so. Can you make it tomorrow evening? Say around five?"

"That will be quite satisfactory."

Jeb provided the directions and said good day. Hector furrowed his brow and looked over at Max, who was now curled atop the Queen Anne sofa table in the living room.

"Well, Max, he certainly didn't sound like someone who would have worded that ad. The mystery deepens. Are you up for a road trip tomorrow?" Max stared at him with inscrutable blue eyes.

Hector spent the remainder of the day at his antique store, Traditions. He and his dear wife, Edna, had established the business fifteen years ago on Rodney Parham Road in Little Rock. It had been touch and go for a while, but Edna possessed excellent business sense and impeccable taste. That, and his willingness to hone his skills and travel to estate sales and auctions in search of quality finds, had enabled them to make the enterprise a success. A varied selection, fair prices, and excellent customer reviews propelled them to a top place in the ratings.

While at the shop, he sold a charming mid-nineteenth century French walnut two-drawer cabinet to a doctor's wife. A favorite piece of his, it had raised panel doors, cabriole legs, inverted finials, and shield-form escutcheons. He hated to see it go — he always hated to see these beautiful pieces leave — but he made a nice profit, which eased the pain, and the doctor's wife was ecstatic.

The next day, he closed his shop early, loaded a protesting Max in his 1953 Bentley sedan, and began the two-hour drive to Hurlin. Hector looked over at his cat. "Sorry, Max. I know traveling is not your cup of tea, but I wouldn't feel right leaving you home when I haven't the slightest idea how long

I'll be gone."

Following Jeb's directions, Hector turned at Jeb's rusting mailbox and traveled down a lane lined with scrub oaks, briars, and weeds. He braked when a covey of bobwhite quail scurried across the road. Soon after, he pulled up in front of a worn, yet well-kept house.

Homer, Jeb's fifty-pound bluetick hound, greeted the arrival with a bawling howl. He raced toward the Bentley, then disappeared from Hector's sight. Two big paws suddenly slammed into the passenger side window, and a large head peered in.

Max, curled up on the seat, jerked his head up in apparent alarm. He arched his back, hissed, and sprang for the highest elevation he could find, Hector's head. Hector yelled and tried to remove the agitated feline, but Max redoubled his efforts to keep his perch. His claws dug in, and a few trickles of blood ran down Hector's face. Jeb came running out of the house, clamped a hand on Homer's collar, and pulled him away from the car. Hector finally dislodged the cat, unceremoniously tossed Max toward the passenger seat, rolled down the car windows an inch or so, and hastily exited the car, slamming the door behind him.

Hector dabbed his face with the starched white handkerchief he always carried, wiping away the drops of blood. That mirror better be worth it, he thought. He peered through the driver's side window to make sure none of the blood had gotten on the car's pristine upholstery, then went around to the passenger side to make sure the wretched dog hadn't left marks on the Bentley's finish. Already, Max was curled in a ball, ready, it seemed, for another nap.

At the same time, Jeb Compton, the owner of the dog and the mirror Hector was anxious to see, was tying his hound, Homer, to a big sycamore tree, then turning to Hector. "Was that a cat I heard a squalling?

"My cat, Max, I'm afraid." He pointed, "That feral dog came out of nowhere and tried to attack him."

Jeb shook his head. "Are you okay? I meant to tie that danged hound up before you got here, but it clean slipped my mind. Just so you know, Homer ain't feral. Just protecting what be his."

Hector touched his scalp and winced. "Good to know. I'm all right, I'm sure. No permanent damage. It was just a bit of a shock."

"Well, I feel bad about it. I got a first aid kit inside if you need it." He stuck out a calloused hand. "We kind of got a bad start, I reckon. Let's you and me try again. I'm Jeb Compton."

Hector shook hands. "Hector Deakins. No need for a first aid kit. My cat Max has had all his shots."

"You still interested in that mirror?"

"Absolutely. I must say, that nicely worded ad certainly caught my attention."

Jeb chuckled. "Can't take no credit for that. Had that lawyer fella come 'round and take a look-see. He knows a bit about them things."

Keeping a watchful eye on Homer, Hector followed Jeb up the steps, onto the weathered oak plank porch, then down a hallway to the living room.

Jeb pointed to the space above the fieldstone fireplace. "There she be."

Hector sucked in his breath and quickly moved to examine the mirror. "Oh, this is exquisite. Definitely from the 1920s. The gilt has hardly flaked or faded. The carving is superb, especially on the Acanthus leaves at the bottom. And look, the mirror's surface shows minimal distressing and no sign of crazing whatsoever, and the beveled edges are sharp and clean."

As Hector continued his enthusiastic description, Jeb's eyes took on the glazed look usually reserved for Reverend Andrews when the good man hit Genesis and commenced on the begats. When he realized that Hector had finally quit talking, Jeb shook his head.

"I'm guessing you like it."

"Like it? It's positively enchanting. Do you happen to know its provenance?"

"Say what, now?"

"Sorry. I mean do you have a record of ownership or the earliest known history?"

Jeb thought about it. "Well, I know my Annie got it from her ma, who got it from hers. Granny brung it with when she come over to the States from France."

"I see. Might your wife know even more about it?"

Jeb flinched. He took a deep breath and looked at Hector with pain-filled eyes. "No doubt she did, but there be no way to ask her now. My Annie passed a few months back."

Hector's mouth fell open. "Oh, I'm so sorry. I had no idea."

"Course you didn't. No reason why you would."

They stood in awkward silence for a moment. "I could use me a beer," Jeb said. "You care to join me?"

Relief showed on Hector's face. "Why, yes. Absolutely."

Jeb led the way to the kitchen, opened the old Westinghouse refrigerator, and removed two bottles of Coors. He pried off the caps with a wall-mounted STARR bottle opener and handed one to Hector.

"Let's set a spell on the porch."

Hector followed Jeb out the door, and they settled in matching white oak rockers. Jeb took a long pull on his beer and stared off into the distance. Hector started to speak but hesitated. He took a swallow of his beer, grimaced, then started in.

"I imagine your wife loved that mirror. It's certainly been maintained in wonderful condition."

"Yes. Annie were always dusting it off or polishing it up." A small smile touched Jeb's lips. "I used to tell her she loved that mirror more than she loved me."

"What did Annie say to that?"

"That she'd been around it longer, and it caused her less aggravation."

Hector laughed. "It sounds like she was quite a woman."

"That she were."

"I hope she didn't suffer much."

"That cancer ate her up in no time. Seems like one minute, she were giving me what-for about something." His eyes teared up, and his voice choked. "And the next, she were gone."

"I'm truly sorry, but if you'll pardon my asking, why are you selling the mirror?"

Jeb stared at Hector. "Why?"

"I mean, don't you want to keep it to remind you of her?"

Fire flared briefly in Jeb's eyes, then died. "Everything in this house reminds me of her. That mirror were her favorite thing, though. When I see it, I think of her, and if I look in her mirror, I see a man who's lost the world."

Hector gazed at Jeb for several seconds. "You could simply take it down and store it someplace."

"I could, but even so, I'd know it were still here. Right now, that mirror be more than I can bear."

Hector nodded, then reached in his vest pocket and took out his billfold. He withdrew a twenty-dollar bill and held it out to Jeb. "Then I'll take it off your hands, sir. On one condition."

Jeb raised his eyebrows, looked at the bill, then back to Hector. "What might that be?"

"If you ever change your mind and want it back, you'll let me know. I shall display it in my shop for my customers to admire, but it will not be for sale."

"You don't have to do that."

"I know, but I want to. Is that agreeable to you?"

Jeb stood up, took the bill, and stuck out his hand. "I reckon so."

They shook on it. Hector got the mirror, wrapped it gently in a blanket, and loaded it in his trunk. He turned the Bentley around in the yard, gave Jeb a wave, and headed toward home.

Jeb untied Homer and patted his head. "Well, Homer, he's a right decent fella for all them fancy words a his." He waved the twenty at Homer. "What say you hop up on the flatbed and we hit the Walmart to stock up on dog food?"

As Hector turned off of Jeb's lane onto the gravel road, he glanced at his cat, who was at that moment stretching. "Well, Max, he's in a bad place right now. I do hope he finds some closure and something to live for. I believe that's what his wife would have wished. I know that's what Edna wanted for me."

# Chapter 4 — Only A Chair

After his Annie died, Jeb Compton made some
adjustments in his morning routine. He slept a little later, ate
things for breakfast frowned upon by Doc Wilkens, and
drank a beer on the porch while he read the daily copy of the
*Hurlin Express*. In addition to the news, the letters to the
editor, and the want ads, he also started checking the
obituaries. If anyone had asked him why, he'd have laughed
and said, "To see if I'm in there." In truth, though, Annie's
passing had schooled him in the fickle nature of life, and in
the obituaries, he found plenty of confirmation.

"Hey, Homer. Leave off that a minute. It say here that
Bessie Lowrey passed away."

Homer, Jeb's big bluetick hound, lay on his back in the
dirt, scratching his back by squirming around. Hearing his
name, he got up, shook himself off, and cocked his head in

Jeb's direction.

"Do you 'member Bessie? She be the one who always gave you a biscuit when we delivered her produce she bought from our garden. Sometimes, she'd even add some sorghum on them biscuits. She were a good and wise soul, and this town be the poorer for her leaving." Jeb stood and tossed the paper on the chair. "I'm glad we got to know her, Homer. Bessie were far more than what they pictured her in the paper."

Formed of worn, white oak and dressed in a flowery print on the padded back and seat cushions, the old rocking chair sat on the porch of the modest old house and seemed incapable of stirring up a fuss. Surely, it could only provide a restful pause on a hot July evening and nothing more.

Sally Lowrey, a slender brunette dressed in a faded denim shirt, Levi jeans, and worn Puma sneakers, stood on the porch. She put her hands on her hips and thrust out her jaw. "I want that chair!"

Elegant in her Pendleton business suit, Jane Evans, her ever-sensible sister, frowned. "Mom asked us to handle this part of Grandma Bessie's estate, Sal, and that's not what we decided. We decided that *all* the furnishings would go in the auction."

"You decided, you mean. Everything else can go — I don't care — but not the chair. It's mine! Grandma left it to me." Jane cocked one perfectly tweezed eyebrow. "She did no such thing."

"Well, she would have if her illness hadn't kept her from changing her will."

"You don't know that. I swear I don't know what gets into

you. Why do you even want that old thing? It's not worth anything."

Despite turning thirty-two in January, Sally had never really outgrown her temper, and Jane's words triggered it. She let it have free reign and dredged up all the contempt she could muster.

"To you! You only think of worth in terms of dollars and cents. Must be the banker in you. And if it's not worth anything, like you say, then it doesn't matter if it's not in the auction."

A flush bloomed on Jane's thin cheeks, and she stamped her foot. "Sally. Mae. Benson!" Each word, flung like a trio of darts, scored a hit, and Sally flinched in spite of herself. "You're impossible, Sally. I can't reason with you when you get like this. That chair's going in the auction, and I'm going back to the motel."

Jane squared her shoulders, spun around, and swiftly descended the steps. The door to her Audi slammed, the engine revved, the tires squealed, and gravel flew as the car peeled out of the driveway.

Sally sighed, walked over to the chair, and sat. It rocked back, finding Sally's center of gravity, and came to a stop. Accompanied by moths flitting around the porch light, the rich, cloying scent of honeysuckle, and the gentle song of the whippoorwills, Sally rocked herself into her memories of her sweet grandma.

Grandma sat in her rocker. It moved gently back and forth while young Sally snuggled in her lap. Grandma softly sang "The Old Rugged Cross" while she stroked the child's hair.

Sally interrupted the singing. "Grandma, what's that song about?"

"Well, Sally, it be about Jesus dying on the cross for our sins."

"But why did he have to die? He didn't do no wrong."

"No, child, He surely did not, but that were the deal He made with his Father so his Father wouldn't punish us sinners."

Sally looked confused. "Shouldn't the sinners be the ones to get punished?"

"God thought so, I reckon, but it seem Jesus saw it different."

"Well, Dad always punishes me when I do something naughty, and Jane never offers to take none of it for me."

Grandma chuckled. "And the other way around, I 'spect. Not too many folks be like Jesus when it comes to sacrificing for someone else's wrong. Don't mean we can't try to be more like Him, though. It's something to think on, ain't it?"

"Yes, Grandma."

Sally's thoughts shifted from her grandma to her sister. Jane could be a real pain in the rear, but she had really made something of herself. She'd become a successful professional, a loan officer at some big bank in Tulsa. She'd married Rick, a nice, good looking, hard-working guy, and they'd had two great kids, Bob and Edith. Everything, it seemed, had worked out well for them.

Sally compared her life to Jane's, and found it didn't measure up — at least by society's standards — but she had no problem with that. She wore no wedding band and planned on keeping it that way. Her parents' nasty divorce had seen to that. That didn't matter, for she enjoyed her own company. She didn't have a high-paying job, a fancy house, or a late-model car, but waitressing over at the Dixie Diner paid the bills and let her meet some nice folk.

Sally suddenly sat straight, jarred from her thoughts by footsteps on the porch stairs. She looked up and saw Jane. Lost within herself, Sally hadn't heard her drive up. She braced herself for another barrel full of angry words, but Jane just stood there and looked at her.

Finally, she spoke. "Why is that chair so important to you?"

Sally started to snap out a sharp reply but found herself unable to deliver one. Maybe the chair had calmed her. Maybe it was the memories of Grandma. And maybe it was a need to explain it to herself as well as to Jane.

"You remember the bad times? What Grandma used to call 'the troubles'?" Sally noticed Jane's mouth, how it had tightened, how she clenched her fists at her sides. Jane didn't speak so Sally continued. "That was when Dad and Mom were fighting before the divorce. They were at each other whenever they were together, and it hurt something fierce to hear it."

"Of course, I remember," Jane said. "It's not something I'm liable to forget."

"Well, when that was going on, you shut everyone out. You stayed in your room, buried yourself in your studies, got a scholarship, and left for college. That's how you got by. I was too young for that, so I came over here. I'd sit on the porch beside Grandma in her rocker, and cry. 'Sally,' she'd say, 'it be okay to cry. It helps to let it out. You're going through a bad patch right now, but there will come a brighter day. Jesus will watch over you, and so will I.' Then she'd put me in her lap and sing to me. She helped me get through it, Jane."

Tears welled in Jane's eyes and escaped down her cheeks. She wiped them away with a quick brush of her silk sleeve. "And the chair?"

"The chair. It's where she always sat to share her wisdom and love. Can't you see why I want it? I can't have her anymore, but —" Sally couldn't continue.

Jane sniffed once. "Well, I suppose that chair doesn't have to go in the auction if it's that important to you. Heaven knows it wouldn't bring that much, anyway."

Sally launched herself out of the rocker and threw her arms around her sister. "Thank you," she whispered. "Thank you."

Jane gave her a quick, awkward hug in return, then stepped back and glanced at her watch. "Goodness, look at the time. The auction's Thursday, and I've still got the inventory to finalize. I'd better get on that. Goodnight, Sally." She fled to her car and drove off.

Sally's throat tightened. "Goodnight, Jane. I love you, too," she said, although Jane hadn't said 'I love you' at all. But Sally knew her sister's language, knew the words that were hardest for her to say. Sally turned and went to load the rocker in her truck.

# Chapter 5 — Decisions

One moment, the big bluetick hound snored blissfully on the porch in the morning sun, and the next, he leaped to his feet and barked. Jeb's shoulders slumped. He stopped walking, laid down his pole and bait bucket, and turned around. "Dang it, Homer, I were trying to sneak off without you noticing. I guess I should a knowed better. Okay, you can come with, but you got to promise me you won't go swimming while I'm a trying to fish."

They headed out, past the small barn, and through the field toward the stock pond. "You know, Homer, I don't get to do this near enough, but I think them soybeans will hold for another hour or so." Homer barked his agreement. "By the way, I heared that Bob Johnson is calling it quits and putting his land up for sale. His kin had that land forever, but I guess he's getting on up there, and it's hard on him to keep working it. It's a nice piece of land. I hope he gets a good price for it."

Jim Archer, a big, burly man, looked out of place in the placid Arkansas meadow. He tromped forward, picking his path to avoid the cow patties, and arrived at a small pond in the heart of the meadow, the same fishing hole Jeb Compton and his dog Homer had visited two weeks before. Jim looked it over. Its steep, muddy banks were dotted with reeds and some scraggly willows.

Nothing much has changed, he thought. Not yet, anyway. He bent to pick up a rock and chucked it into the water. Red-eared sliders, sunning on a log, their turtle bodies looking like army helmets, slid into the water. A large bullfrog croaked and leaped from the bank. Jim watched the ripples radiate outward from the frog's point of entry. A memory tugged: concentric circles. That's what his old geometry teacher had called them.

He had skipped rocks on this pond in years past, often when he was doing his best thinking. He found a flat rock and pegged it at the surface. Two hops. He scratched his ear and then remembered he had to keep his elbow tucked and throw sidearm. He tried again. Five hops.

"Not bad, Mister." Jim's head jerked toward the voice. It belonged to a redheaded boy of twelve or so. The boy was sunburned, barefoot, and clad in worn overalls and a threadbare flannel shirt. A long, cane pole rested on one shoulder, and he carried a Folgers coffee can full of bait.

"Yeah, well, it's been a long time. I see you're going to do some fishing."

"Sure am. I'm after Old Jake."

"Old Jake? Is he still —"

If the boy noticed Jim's abrupt halt, he gave no sign.

"He's a catfish, Mister. Biggest old cat in these parts, I'll bet. He's been in that pond forever."

Forever? Jim thought. Bit of a stretch, but it's certainly been at least a dozen years.

"Yeah? Well, I hope you get him."

The boy grinned. "Me too, but it ain't likely. The only time I ever hooked him, he snapped my line. Won't happen again, though. I'm using fifty-pound test now. You like to fish, Mister?"

Man, Jim thought, this kid's a talker. "I used to when I was your age. When you grow up, there's not much time for such things. There's always work to be done and money to be made."

The boy's grin faltered. "Say, you mind if I ask you something, Mister?"

"Shoot."

"Well, if you ain't here to fish, why are you here?"

Jim's mouth tightened in a hard line. He didn't have to account for himself, especially not to some kid he just met. He almost said as much, but looking at the boy's freckled, friendly face, he opted for the truth. "I'm trying to decide about something."

The boy didn't say anything, but his eyes held open curiosity. "I'm trying to decide what to do with this meadow."

The boy looked puzzled. "What do you mean, Mister? This land belongs to old Bob Johnson."

"Not anymore. I bought it from him last week."

The boy's blue eyes widened. "Really? Gee, is it still okay for me to fish?"

"Sure, kid."

Relief spread over the boy's face, and Jim shook his head.

People are the same at any age, Jim thought. When something surprises them, they think first about how it will affect them.

Yeah, look out for number one. Words to live by. The boy plopped down on the muddy bank, baited his hook with an uncooperative nightcrawler, and tossed his line in the water. The plastic bobber rocked for a moment, then stilled. He pushed the base of the pole into the soft earth and propped it up with a rock, a tactic that let him fish hands-free. Satisfied with his efforts, he looked at Jim.

"Mister?"

"Yeah?"

"You said you're trying to figure what to do with the meadow. Does that mean you ain't going to use it to keep cows or grow hay?"

"I run a construction company, kid. There's not much call for cows and hay in my line of work."

A frown creased the boy's forehead. "Construction. That's building things, right?"

"Right."

The boy's frown deepened. "And building things means tearing up the land with them dozers and stuff?"

Jim raised his eyebrows. Where's he going with this? he wondered.

"Well, yes. When we've got to get a building site ready, clearing the land is necessary."

The boy didn't reply right away. He stared at the bobber and scratched a chigger bite on his ankle. Then he looked up at Jim. "Are you planning to build in the meadow?"

No flies on this kid, Jim thought. "Maybe. The city's talking about putting up a shopping center, and this meadow's in a good location."

"Do they have to put it here?"

"No, but I'll make a profit if they buy the land from me, and my company's got a good shot at the building contracts."

The boy worked a stone loose from the bank. He sat still, turning it over, then stood and pitched it far into the meadow. With tears in his eyes and fists clenched at his sides, he turned and faced Jim. "It ain't right, Mister!

Jim blinked. "Hey, kid, why're you getting so upset?"

"Don't it bother you that this meadow will get all tore up just so folks can have some fancy place to shop?"

Jim's ears reddened. "Now just a minute, kid," he said, his voice booming. "I didn't say I was building here — just that I was thinking about it. This is my land now, and I can do whatever I want with it."

The boy was not cowed by Jim's anger. He looked ready to continue his attack, but then he turned and stared at the pond. Jim followed his gaze and sucked in his breath. The bobber wasn't visible, the cane pole bent almost double, and the line raced back and forth like a fly in a bottle.

"It's Old Jake, Mister! It's gotta be."

The boy ran to the pole and pulled it from the ground. It almost came free from his grasp, but he held tight. He tried to back up, but the slippery bank gave him no traction. Each backward step resulted in a slide forward. "Mister, I need help!"

Jim ran over to the boy. He gripped the pole, placing his hands above and below the boy's, and pulled. The strain was incredible. Slowly, slipping and sliding, they backed up until forty-pounds of furious catfish flopped on the bank with croaking protests. The boy's voice was hushed and reverent. "We did it, Mister. We landed Old Jake."

Jim wiped the sweat from his forehead with the back of

his hand. "We sure did, kid. What are you going to do with him?"

The boy stood, brows knitted in thought. "I reckon I'll let him go."

Jim's mouth fell open. "After all this time trying to catch him, why would you let him go?"

"Well, I figure if you're gonna build in the meadow, he ain't long for this world. He may as well spend his last days where he's happy."

The boy watched as Jim pulled a jackknife from his hip pocket and walked toward the fish. "I'm gonna cut the line, but I'll leave the hook in his bony old jaw. It won't hurt him none, but it will give him something to help him remember this tussle."

"Wait a minute."

The boy turned around.

"What's your name, kid?"

"Tommy Jenkins."

"Well, Tommy, you can let Old Jake go if you want to, but I'm thinking maybe this meadow wouldn't make such a great place for a shopping center after all. Maybe cows, or hay, or some such might be the way to go. What do you think?"

Tommy smiled, the kind of smile that could not be measured in dollars and cents. It seemed to radiate off the water, casting light across the meadow, and all the way into Jim's happy heart.

# Chapter 6 — All's Fair At The Fair

Anticipated by the young and old, the yearly Hurlin Fair started the third Monday of September and ran for a week. Kids would wander wide-eyed down a midway strewn with the flashing lights and bells of arcade games, whirling rides with musical accompaniment, and animal shows featuring gators, racing pigs, and such. Fair-goers would gorge themselves on popcorn, cotton candy, funnel cakes, nachos, and hot dogs, which they sometimes expelled after a particularly unsettling ride. Young men would try to win a stuffed animal for their girls or take them on the Ferris wheel where there would be a chance to steal a kiss. Grownups would listen to country bands, especially if the fair committee managed to snag a halfway major name, inspect livestock on display, and check out the crafts, produce entries, and homemade pies and cakes that were up for ribbons.

Jeb Compton had no idea that he was about to play a role in this year's fair when he checked his morning mail and one letter caught his attention.

"Hey, Homer, guess what?" Jeb called out.

The big bluetick hound reluctantly left off his hot pursuit of a chattering blue jay and turned his attention to Jeb, who held up a letter. "Seems the fair committee wants me to be a judge for them folks as has entered the baked goods competition. What do you make of that?"

Homer glanced back at that ornery jay that was eyeing him from a nearby tree and chuffed out a sigh. He looked back at Jeb and did his best to look interested.

"Annie used to judge baked goods at the fair every year. Now, Homer, I used to tell her she ought to step away and enter her own self, but she always shushed me. Annie never thought her baking were up to snuff, but what I wouldn't give for another taste of just one crumb of her cooking again. I reckon they is asking me to judge as a sign of respect to her. Can't very well say no in that case. 'Sides, I don't mind tasting them cakes and pies neither."

Bertie Mae Johnson's sweet potato pie won Grand Champion in the baked goods division for three years running. That in itself was no small thing, and if she had just shown a little dab of humility, few folks would have begrudged her success. But Bertie Mae and humility had never become acquainted.

Emma Claudell was not happy. A thin stick of a woman with short brown hair, close-set eyes, and a scowl that could back off a badger, she spoke her mind in the knitting circle where Bertie Mae was the current topic of conversation.

"Well, sir," Emma said, "I'm plumb sick of her crowing about her danged pies! Every time I see her, she works the talk around to them and that special plate she always puts them on. Now that the fair's opening in four days, it be even worse."

There were general nods of agreement among three of the ladies, but Becky Flynn, a redhead with curls and a sweet smile — but a pinch of the Devil inside her — spoke up. "Now, Emma, could it be you're just tired of lagging behind?"

The alpha female's nostrils flared, and her eyeballs bulged a tad. "That don't make no never mind," Emma said. "'Sides, anybody with a lick of sense knows my pies be every bit as good as hers."

She glared around the circle, daring anyone to disagree. Several were probably thinking about pointing out that past judges likely saw it differently, but the pack cowered and was silent. Even Becky held her tongue. Emma should have stopped there, but she was on a roll. "And I'll tell y'all something else. This time's going be different. Yes sir, this be the year when *my* pie takes the top prize, and I get *my* picture in the *Hurlin Express*."

That evening, Emma sat in her hard-backed chair under the ceiling fan in her small living room and simmered. It's not that she had a mean spirit, she thought. She just couldn't abide a braggart like Bertie. But Emma knew she'd said too much earlier and her words had all but tied a noose around her neck.

If she didn't beat Bertie this year, she would be a laughing stock. She turned it over every which way but could see no way out of her fix. Truth be told, she knew Bertie's pies were better than hers, even though she'd said publicly they weren't. She couldn't change that. She thought her pie's

41

insides and outside appearance measured up to Bertie's. It was the difference in flavor that cost her.

Emma's head jerked upright, an idea forming in her fevered mind. A smile that would give a gator pause touched her thin lips. Well then, she thought, if I can't outbake her, then I'll just have to go another route. She stood up, went over to the rotary phone on her coffee table, and dialed Sarah Grimes of the fair committee.

"Hey, Sarah, this is Emma Claudell. I know folks got to get their fair entries in this Saturday afternoon, but I'm wondering what's the time frame. 1:00 p.m. to 5:00 p.m.? Thank you. And the results will be ready by Monday's opening, right? Good enough."

After forcing herself to exchange a few pleasantries, even asking about Sarah's brats, she ended the conversation and placed the phone's handset back in its cradle. This is perfect, she thought. If I know Bertie, she'll have her pie in as soon as she can. I just need to take mine in a bit later.

Emma spent time the next morning, an already hot and humid Friday, shopping for the ingredients needed for her baking. She went to the grocery store and two produce stands before she found sweet potatoes to her liking. At one of the antique malls, she found the plate she was looking for. It were a bit pricey, she thought, but it would be worth it. Then she headed home. It would take her several hours to get everything ready.

Back in her kitchen, Emma boiled the sweet potatoes whole in their skins for forty-five minutes. She then ran cold water over them and removed their skins. She broke apart the sweet potatoes in a bowl, added butter, and mixed with a wooden spoon. She stirred in a cup of sugar, a half cup of milk, two eggs, a half teaspoon each of ground nutmeg and cinnamon, and one teaspoon of vanilla, and attacked the mixture with an egg beater until the mixture smoothed out. Pouring the filling into the required nine-inch unbaked pie crust, she baked the pie in the oven at three-hundred-fifty degrees for an hour. The pie puffed up like a souffle, then gradually sank down as it cooled. When it was ready, she carefully placed it on the plate she had purchased and covered it with cellophane. Emma slept well that night and dreamed of victory.

Saturday afternoon, around 3:00 p.m., found Emma and her pie at the registration desk in the exhibit hall. After getting her assigned number, and her ID tag filled out and attached with tape to her pie, she walked a short distance to look at the quilt entries. If asked, she couldn't have said what any one of them looked like, since her gaze remained locked on the woman placing Emma's pie with the others.

When the crowd grew and the volunteers became busier, Emma strolled over to the baked goods table and found Bertie's entry. It was sitting close to hers, and as she'd hoped, they looked identical, right down to the plates they rested on. Perfect, she thought. Emma scanned the crowd, saw her opportunity, and quickly switched the tags. She took a quick turn around the room, trying to seem interested in the exhibits, then left and headed home.

Emma could barely contain herself that Sunday as she waited for the fair to open to the public. When Monday arrived, she drove to the fairgrounds, parked her Plymouth, paid her fifty-cent entry fee, and hurried over to enter the exhibit hall. Ignoring the racks of photographs, the wall display of art, the quilts hanging on lines and draped over folding tables, the flower arrangements, and the jars of preserved fruits and vegetables, Emma made a beeline for the table that displayed the winners.

She elbowed her way through the crowd in front of her

and eagerly scanned for the pie with the big purple ribbon with the gold State of Arkansas seal on the circle up top. Spotting it, she edged closer, read the attached tag, and her world collapsed. Printed neatly on the entry tag was the name Bertie Mae Johnson.

Emma's mouth fell open, and she gaped like a carp flopping on the bank. That don't make no sense, she thought. Bertie's pie had my entry tag on it, and Bertie's pies always win. Which means I should have won. What in the Sam Hill is going on?

Her legs trembled. She felt like sinking to the floor, but somehow, she staggered over to the desk where Sarah Grimes sat. Emma took a deep breath.

"Hey, Sarah. Who were the judge on the baked goods this year?"

"Oh, it was Jeb Compton. He did a nice job for us."

Emma fought to keep her composure. "I see Bertie Mae won again with her pie. Did Jeb have anything to say about it?"

"Matter of fact, he did. He said it tasted just like the pies his Annie used to bake."

# Chapter 7 — Hambone

Homer loped into Jeb's yard, bawling like a banshee. He'd been making his morning rounds, and just then shot up on the porch where Jeb usually sat in the early hours of the day, plopped his rear down in front of him, and began frantically pawing at his nose. Jeb rose and approached the big hound who whined in misery.

He inspected Homer and shook his head. "Homer, you got yourself into a patch of stinging nettle. The hairs on that stuff is nasty for sure. Come over here with me."

Jeb led the hound to the outdoor faucet where he ran cold water from the hose over Homer's snout for several minutes.

"That should cool down the burning some, but it be a temporary fix. I need to go over to that patch of nettles and see if I can find me some jewelweed nearby. You stay right here and do your best not to paw at it. I'll be back soon as I can."

Homer lay by the faucet, whimpering. A while later, Jeb returned, holding a plant with oval, round-toothed leaves. He cut off the roots of the jewelweed with his pocket knife, then rubbed the oozing stalks over Homer's muzzle. "That should ease the itching and swelling. Let that dry a minute, while I get some calamine lotion from the bathroom."

He returned shortly with a bottle and some cotton. He sponged Homer's muzzle liberally with the calamine-soaked cotton. Soon Homer's muzzle turned a fine shade of pink.

"That's the best I can do for you right now, my friend. If that don't get it, I'll get you some aloe vera. And if you ain't better by tomorrow, we'll swing by the vet." Homer cocked his head like he understood every word and appreciated Jeb's attention. Jeb rubbed Homer's chest before he sat down, picked up the dropped copy of the *Hurlin Express,* and resumed reading.

"Hey, Homer, it say here that our neighbor, Bob Thornton, passed away. I hate to hear that, but I knew he'd been a ailing. When we checked on him awhile back, he seemed to be on the mend. I declare, Homer, you just never know, now do you?

"Bob were a good man, and he never complained once when you strayed over on his property." Jeb shook his head, remembering the first time he met Bob down at the feed store, back when Jeb first moved to Hurlin. Bob had been telling a story about a cow that got loose, running through the long johns that hung on the clothesline, and he'd bent over double, laughing at his own dilemma.

"He sure could spin a yarn," Jeb said to Homer. "I'll have to go to the funeral and pay my respects." Jeb rubbed his chin. "I wonder who's going to inherit his house and land. Seems I remember him telling me once that he had a brother somewhere in the state. Guess we'll find out in due time."

Howdy, journal. My name's Hambone. It's not, of course, but that's what I go by around here. I'm here to tell you about myself because Pa thought it a good idea to get my thoughts on paper. Why, I have no idea, but if you knew my pa, you'd know there's no point in arguing with him. So, here I am, about to commence as best I can. Since I mentioned Pa, I guess that's as a good point as any to start.

Pa has him a stubborn streak a mile wide. That's all I can figure for why he hung on to these miserable acres of land in northwest Arkansas. For more years than he'd probably care to remember, he tried to coax a decent crop of anything from that poor, rocky soil. He'd likely be there still, fighting and cussing that land, if his brother Bob hadn't died and left him his spread down in Hurlin.

My, oh, my, he's stubborn. It's why Pa fathered us four girls, or so Ma claimed. Apparently his family brought him up believing that a man needed to pass on the family name. Since he needed a son for that, Ma explained, he planned to keep trying till he got one. When Ma finally wore down and died three years after giving birth to me, his plans got derailed.

I reckon he could have remarried and kept trying, but best I could tell, Ma's passing seemed to break something inside of him and he just gave up on the idea. Frustrated in his goal, he settled on the next best thing: he raised me and my older sisters — Sam, Pat, and Ash — as boys. On my birth certificate, my name is Dorothy, but I guess he couldn't work a way to turn that into the male gender. So, in a fit of spite, maybe, I became Hambone.

When the powers that be told Pa that he needed to enroll us in school, Pa had none of that. He told them he would school us himself, and I guess they got tired of arguing with him. It's not that he didn't believe in a good education. "Didn't I make it clean through the eighth grade?" he often asked us. It's just he felt he could do the job himself. So, Pa taught us the three Rs (reading, writing, arithmetic) while concentrating on the fundamentals he deemed most important: farming, fishing, and fighting. He dubbed them the three Fs, and they served us well in our lives.

Pa didn't shelter us from the world, neither. Every Sunday, we'd go to church at a small, hillside chapel near town. There were trips to the market, as well as to the roadside stands selling fresh fruits and vegetables. Ever so often, there'd be a fair, and Pa often swung us by the little town library to check out some reading. Once in a while, Pa would haul us to a city council meeting to have his say on some matter, and he gave them what-for on more than one occasion.

As a coming of age ritual, he taught each of us to drive in a beat-up brown '64 Ford truck as soon as our feet could reach the peddles. By the time I got my turn there wasn't much life left in the old girl. She had a stick shift on the floor, and the transmission had one missing gear. I worked hard to give that missing gear a companion, and the crickets often paused to admire the grinding sounds I coaxed out of her.

I swear that old truck might have been the only thing I've met more stubborn than Pa. With four rowdy girls taking turns at the wheel, it's a miracle she made it as long as she did. I guess pride and a sense of duty kept her together till she'd completed her job and we'd learned.

That truck still decorates the field we left her in when she gave her last gasp — a monument to trials taken and passed. We held a service for her, and each said a few words, and I swear I saw Pa tear up a couple of times.

I sometimes wonder if that red ribbon we put on her hood is still there. It marked our way of paying respect to a true and faithful companion. If I talked more about that old truck than I do about the boys I'll mention, it's because I understood the truck. Boys are still a great mystery to me.

We grew faster than the sweet corn in our garden, and at some point, boys started noticing us and coming around. With Pa holding court, we knew each suitor would have to pass muster before receiving his blessing. More than one failed the test and got sent packing. Still, they kept coming. Sam, the pretty one, with her long blonde hair and devil-may-care eyes, left us first. She got hitched to Lem Dawkins from the farm a few fields over. Then came Pat, the sweet brown-haired one with the caring disposition. She got hitched to John Johnston. Next came Ash, with her glossy black hair and spunky, no-nonsense attitude. She got hitched to Ralph Pearson. And that left me.

With my wild, dishwater blonde hair that wouldn't be tamed, and my freckled nose and gangly limbs, I sometimes despaired of any boy in his right mind ever wanting me. I wasn't pretty. I wasn't real smart. My nature wasn't the sweetest — I had a habit of speaking my mind, for instance. But Pa, in his infinite wisdom, knew better. "You've turned seventeen now, Hambone, and your time's coming. You got a lot more going for you than you know, and you'll find someone right for you. The good ones up here is about used up, anyway. Maybe some fresh territory will provide what you need." He was talking about our move to his departed brother's place in Hurlin.

Truth is, I knew Pa no longer possessed the vigor of his

youth. His pace had slowed, and he couldn't tend his farm like before. I figured he'd likely need some help in moving across the state and establishing himself in a new place, so I didn't mind waiting. We sold the farm for more than I would have expected — there were some land developers who fancied it for some reason and paid good money. We packed up what we could, loaded up a big U-Haul Pa had rented, and bid goodbye to the only home I'd ever known.

And so we came to Hurlin, here in Garland County. It stood a far piece from our old homestead, but I felt a growing excitement as we passed the city limits sign. We stopped at a gas station — a two-pump Standard — in town, filled up and got directions to Uncle Bob's place, God rest his soul.

As we pulled up to the spread, we took in the surroundings. After we got out, the first thing Pa did was head over to the garden. He knelt down, scooped up a handful of soil, squeezed it, and let it slowly trickle out between his fingers. The look of utter joy on his face was a wonder to behold. He got up, dusted his hands off, and we walked all around the place, Pa exclaiming at this and that.

"Look at this. This here barn is well-built and sturdy. It wasn't here last time I visited. You wouldn't remember, Hambone. It must have been better than twenty-five years ago when me and your mama visited Bob." Pa craned his neck to see the loft. "We can store a mess of hay in that loft." We walked outside, and Pa said, "Look at that. This chicken coop is real nice. Can't wait to stock it with hens and a rooster. We'll have us some fresh eggs."

Our inspection got interrupted by the sound of a vehicle coming down our lane. As it approached, I spotted a Ford flatbed truck with a tall man behind the wheel and a big hound in the passenger seat. The truck pulled up behind our U-Haul and parked, and the occupants came out and walked toward us. The man shook hands with Pa and introduced himself to us as Jeb Compton. "And this here's Homer."

Pa knelt down and patted the hound. "I'm James, Bob Thornton's brother. And this is my daughter, Hambone."

Mr. Compton tipped his hat to me. If my name threw him off, he didn't act like it. "Sure sorry to hear about Bob," he said. "He were a fine man and a good neighbor. If y'all need anything, just give me a holler." Mr. Compton pointed. "I live at the second farm you come to if is you was traveling south."

Pa stood up. "Thank you kindly," he said. "Bob was a mite older than me. Always trying to look after me when I was a kid. Seems like he's looking after me still."

Pa's eyes watered some, and it seemed like Homer the hound figured he could help some. He leaned against Pa's leg like he still wanted to get petted. "Your dog sure is a dandy," Pa said. "Why don't you let the old boy off the leash? Let him run around a bit."

Jeb frowned. "I don't know about that. Sometimes he acts a mite rowdy." Pa told him it'd be fine, so Jeb let Homer loose.

The hound made a beeline to me, reared up on his hind legs, put two huge paws on my shoulders, and gave me a sloppy kiss. I didn't fall down, but the weight of that dog had me straining something fierce. Pa proved no help as he was doubled up with laughter, but Mr. Compton came running over and hauled Homer off of me.

"I'm sure sorry, Miss. I should a knowed better. This hound just can't help hisself."

I told him no harm done, and I knelt down and hugged the big hound.

As Jeb and Pa got to know each other, Homer and I continued exploring the property. After a while, we returned, and they were still deep in conversation. I'd never seen Pa talk that long a spell with anyone. To me, it looked like they were well on the way to becoming fast friends.

And so, one big part of my story ends, and another part begins here in Hurlin. I have to say I have high hopes for the future. Maybe someday, when I see how it plays out, I'll tell you all about it.

# CHAPTER 8 — HOMER GETS HIS COMEUPPANCE

While taking a pull from his first beer of the morning, Jeb sat in the old wicker chair on his front porch and scanned the classified ads in the *Hurlin Express*. One ad jumped out at him like a cat escaping bathwater. He set his bottle down on the porch and read the ad again.

> **FAINTING GOATS FOR SALE —**
> **Young Does: $25. Young Bucks:**
> **$17. Not for sale as meat goats!**
> **Call 831-2664. Ask for John.**

Jeb removed his sweat-stained John Deere cap and ran his hand through his hair. Fainting goats? he thought. He'd never heard of such. What on earth would make a goat faint?

"What do you think, Homer?" This was directed to his bluetick coonhound who lazed on the porch in the morning sun. Homer whimpered in his sleep. His legs jerked in pinwheel fashion, and his claws scrabbled on the old oak planks.

Hearing no wise counsel forthcoming, Jeb decided there was but one way to satisfy his curiosity. Rising from his chair, newspaper clutched in hand and beer bottle forgotten, he entered the house through the door leading to his hallway. He took the first left into the kitchen, picked up the handset of the rotary phone on the counter, and dialed the number. A woman's voice answered; he gave his name and asked for John.

"I'm sorry, but John went to the store. May I take a message?

"Well, ma'am, I seen his ad in today's paper, and I wanted to ask him some questions about them goats."

Her voice grew colder by several degrees, and Jeb could imagine frost forming on the handset. "I have nothing to do with those creatures. It's Jeb, right? Shall I take your number and have him call you?"

Jeb mulled that over. "I'm in and out myself, and I ain't got one of them answering machines, so it might be best if I could drop by."

"Very well. Do you know where Military Road is?"

"Is that off of Highway 49?"

"Yes. We're about five miles out on the left. Look for a two-story house near a barn and stock pond. I'll tell him to expect you."

"Thank you kindly." Jeb put down the handset and retraced his path to the porch. "Are you up for a little trip, Homer?"

Homer opened his eyes, stood up, shook himself hard enough to almost take him off his feet, then bounded off the porch and onto the flat bed of Jeb's '70 Ford F250 truck. He plopped his bottom down between two hay bales and looked at Jeb expectantly.

"I'm coming, old son. Just hold your horses."

Jeb crossed the yard and climbed into the cab. He turned the key in the ignition, and after a few misfires, the engine caught and held. He steered out of his front yard, drove down his country lane, then turned onto the eight-mile stretch of gravel road that led to Highway 49. Homer stuck his head over the side where the wind would flap his jowls and create a slobber hazard for anyone following too closely. About thirty minutes later, they arrived at their destination.

Jeb exited the truck and looked around. A spectacled younger man — in his mid-thirties by Jeb's reckoning — came through the pasture gate and stuck out his hand. "Hello. You must be Jeb. I'm John Winston."

Jeb shook John's hand, noticing that it was not callused like his own. "Howdy."

John started to say something else, but he was interrupted by a blood-curdling howl. Homer leaped off the truck, ran over to John and commenced sniffing him in the crotch. John took a quick step back.

Jeb shot his hand out and grabbed Homer's collar, hauling him back. "Homer! Mind your manners." Homer looked not a whit embarrassed. "Sorry about that," Jeb said. "That just be a bluetick's way of greeting a stranger. He don't mean nothing by it."

John looked a shade paler. He swallowed once and cast a glance at Homer as if to assess Jeb's grip on the collar. "That's quite all right, I'm sure. Splendid looking animal. Now then, my wife tells me you have some questions about my

55

goats."

"Yessir, I do. I ain't never heared of no fainting goats. What that be about?"

John's eyes lit up. "It's a wonderful breed; I wrote my doctoral dissertation on them. I teach at the college and raise them on the side. They're thought to have been originally brought to Tennessee from Nova Scotia in the 1880s."

"Huh. Well, that's real interesting, but what's this fainting business?"

"Oh, they don't actually faint. I mean, their leg muscles do seize up and cause them to fall over, but they stay conscious the whole time. It's a muscle condition called *myotonia congenita.* It's hereditary and congenital."

Jeb scratched his head with his free hand. "Do tell. But what causes them goats to do that in the first place?"

"Oh, it can be a variety of things. A sudden, unfamiliar noise, for example. Or really, anything that scares or startles them."

"Huh. Well, all I know about goats is they eat about anything, give head butts, and stand around on top of things."

John laughed. "Oh, my goats do all that. They just have this extra ability. Do you want to see them?"

"Sure do. Let me tie this pesky dog up first."

Half-walking, half-pulling Homer over to the truck, Jeb got a piece of rope and fastened him to the door handle. "Now stay out of trouble while I'm gone." Homer looked at him reproachfully. Jeb rejoined John, and they walked through the pasture gate and headed toward the barn. Once they got close, Jeb saw a small herd of goats milling around the barnyard. Some were feeding at a trough. A few stood on bales of hay. Two young males were butting heads.

"They don't look none too unusual to me."

"Oh, not to the casual eye, but there are differences. They're a bit smaller than standard goats. Their ears are larger and wider than Swiss goats but smaller and less saggy than Spanish goats. Their eyes are large and protruding. They're less likely to climb fences because of their condition. They make wonderful pets. And, of course, they, for lack of a better word, do faint."

Jeb gave a low whistle. "Land sakes, you sure do know your goats."

John smiled. "Well, they are an enthusiasm of mine." His expression turned wistful. "One I wish my wife shared. She's the reason I have to sell them."

Jeb thought back to his phone conversation with the woman and felt a tug of sympathy for the young man. He remembered his own dear Annie, gone for a year now. There were sure times when she had no truck with some of his pursuits, and she never held back from letting him know about it. He wondered if he should say something.

Best not, Jeb thought. He don't know me from Adam, and I doubt he'd care to hear none of my opinions on the matter.

"So, can I see them goats faint?"

John frowned. "I'm afraid not. They're kind of special to me, and I don't like to upset them."

Jeb considered. "Well, I can respect that, but it do bring up a question."

"What's that?"

"Your wanting to sell them goats, and your billing them as being the fainting kind."

"So?"

"So, how do folks know they be the real thing if they can't see them faint?"

John stared at him. "I never thought of that."

The silence that descended was shattered by a loud bawl

as Homer rounded the corner and came barreling toward them. The goats scattered, but they didn't get far. Their legs seized up and most toppled over like ten-pins in a bowling alley. Some fell on their sides. Others rolled over on their backs with their legs straight up in the air. A few didn't fall but ran awkwardly on locked legs.

Jeb managed to snag Homer by his collar. The whole episode was over in fifteen seconds or so as the goats regained control of their limbs and went about their business.

Jeb glared at Homer who stared at the goats with rapt attention. "I'm dang sorry about that. I'd a swore I had him tied up good. Is them goats all right?"

John had clamped both hands to his head, but he lowered his arms and took a deep breath. "Yes, they're fine. They don't experience any physical pain from the trauma, so no real harm done." He gave a weak laugh. "At least now you know they're the real deal."

"I reckon I do. Dangest thing I ever did see."

"So, you think you might be interested in purchasing one?"

"Well, now."

John quickly added, "I should mention that they're quite social animals. If you just get one, it will tend to look for another animal for companionship."

Jeb raised his eyebrows. "Another animal?"

His eyes went to Homer. "Might that other animal be an aggravating hound?"

"Oh, yes. But I should warn you that the goat would probably follow him around and pester him to death."

Jeb smiled. "Well, sir, I think we can work a deal."

## CHAPTER 9 — MISFIRE

Jeb Compton sat on his porch sipping his morning Coors and leafing through the *Hurlin Express* while his big bluetick lazed by his feet. "Hey, Homer, it say here that Jim Brown's adding another agent to his staff. That insurance outfit's sure be growing leaps and bounds. Jim did a crackerjack job for Annie and me when we needed a new roof after that big storm some years back. Got us fixed right up and didn't hike up our premiums neither.

Jeb smiled at his hound. "You'd a enjoyed that, Homer — getting to bark at the roofer and chase after them old shingles he tossed down. I'm glad Jim and his wife Sarah come to Hurlin. They is good folk."

Sarah Brown sat on the over-stuffed paisley sofa, her legs tucked beneath her, and twirled a lock of her auburn hair. Turning forty and stuck in Hurlin, she thought. Neither is my idea of a good time. I thought I'd finally escaped this place, but the vacuum of fate played one of its cruel little jokes and sucked me right back in. Can't be helped, though. Jim did so well in Little Rock that he got assigned here to run the Farmers Insurance branch, and time took care of the rest.

At least I'll get to go out to celebrate, she thought. She planned the evening in her mind. We'll drive over to Hot Springs and eat at a fancy restaurant — maybe Rolando's. Then we'll take in a movie, or maybe go dancing, or take an evening stroll down The Grand Promenade, a scenic walk that would take them past the city's renowned old bathhouses. When we get back home, we'll get ready for bed and —

The ringing phone interrupted her thoughts. Letting loose a sigh, she uncurled her body, stood up, and walked to the kitchen to answer. "Brown residence."

"Hi, birthday girl. What you up to?"

I'm up to forty, she thought. "Hi, Rhonda. Just sitting around before I go wash up the dishes."

"Sounds like fun. Is the dishwasher on the fritz again?"

"Yeah. Same old, same old."

"Maybe Jim will get you a new one for your birthday."

"No. Our extended policy with Sears is still in effect, so we're trying to squeeze a bit more from the old girl. Besides, he'll give me jewelry."

"How do you know?"

"He's given me jewelry on my birthday every single year since we've been married."

Rhonda paused. "Sounds kind of predictable."

Sarah's voice sharpened. "Hey, I like jewelry. It's what I

always ask for."

Rhonda laughed. "Well, I guess a gal can't have too much of that. So, how does it feel to be forty?"

"Hmm, let me think about that for a minute."

Sarah looked in the tall mirror mounted near the phone. The reflected image showed a reasonably smooth complexion. She had the beginnings of crow's feet around her blue eyes and lines at the corners of her mouth, and a hint of a double chin presented itself. A stray lock of brown hair dangled down her forehead, and she pushed it back in place. She finished her inspection. All in all, she thought, there's no major wear and tear. It wouldn't hurt to shed a few pounds. As she continued to gaze in the mirror, her mind drifted.

Only eleven years old, Sarah bounced into the trailer where she lived, a clutch of wildflowers she'd found by the nearby highway in her hand, to wish her mom a happy birthday. Her mom, Edna, sprawled on her bed in her robe. Tears flowed down her cheeks, creating runnels in her makeup. She clutched a half-empty bottle of Jim Beam in her left hand, no glass visible.

"I feel like crap."

Sarah handed her mother the flowers: white yarrow, the bright red spike of Indian paintbrush, but her mom refused to take them. "What's wrong, Mom?"

Edna looked at Sarah like it was obvious. "I'm forty."

"Is that a bad thing to be?"

Edna sneered at her. "A woman should just hang it up when she turns forty. Makeup only hides things for so long. Men notice soon enough and go sniffing around younger women. That's what your pa did. Then he left us."

Edna's final words in her tear-filled, alcohol-fueled lecture burned themselves into Sarah's memory. "If you ever marry, Sarah, find a man who won't leave you when you're showing signs of aging. Find one you can know inside out and depend on. Now go away, and leave me alone."

"Sarah? Are you still there?"

"Oh, sorry. My mind drifted for a little bit."

She looked at her watch. "I'd better get cracking, Rhonda. Jim will be home soon, and I've got to finish getting ready."

"Okay. Have a great time tonight."

Sarah stood by the living room window and watched as her husband's 1973 AMC Gremlin pulled in the driveway. She shook her head. That car, she thought. It's perfect for Jim: a little quirky and not too flashy, but ultimately solid and dependable. Definitely a keeper.

He came in, looked her up and down, and whistled appreciatively. "Honey, you look great! You about ready to hit the road?"

Sarah smiled. "After that greeting, how could I not be good to go?"

They parked the car in the lot and entered Rolando's, Jim carrying a shoe-box sized package under one arm. They were seated and given menus. "What looks good, honey?" Jim said.

"I think I'll have the Pescado De Mesias."

"Excellent choice, ma'am," said the waiter who suddenly

appeared at their table. "And for you, sir?"

"I'm going to go with the Pollo Bohemio."

"Very good, sir. And to drink?" Sarah ordered a white wine and Jim a Cerveza. As they dined, Sarah looked around. She admired the golden walls formed of crumbling plaster. The lovely murals were said to have been hand-carved by Rolando himself. The black tablecloths added elegance, and the massive wooden beams spoke to her of longevity and strength. I love it here, she thought, and the Central and South American food is so good. It's sure a far cry from the Dixie Diner.

After dessert — the white chocolate cheesecake for Sarah and the Caribbean Rum Cake for Jim — they leaned back in their chairs. Sarah looked at Jim. "Great meal. Only one thing could make it better."

Jim cocked an eyebrow. "Hmm? And what might that be?" He followed Sarah's gaze, which had homed in on the present placed on an adjacent chair. "Oh, I'd almost forgotten about that." He grinned at her frown, reached for the box, and presented it to her with a flourish. "Happy birthday, honey."

Sarah restrained herself from tearing off the wrapping, thinking the bigger box was a ploy. Surely Jim had gotten her the bracelet she'd talked to him about no less than a dozen times. Once the wrapping paper came off, she opened the box and stared at the contents: a pair of pink and white shoes. She looked blankly at Jim. "What is this?"

"Athletic shoes, honey. The latest ones Nike makes. I thought the colors would suit you. Do you like them?"

Her voice raised. "But it's not jewelry. You always give me jewelry!"

"I know, but I don't want you thinking I'm too predictable."

Sarah looked like he'd slapped her. She pushed back her

chair, leaped to her feet, and rushed out of the restaurant in tears. Stunned, Jim sat for a moment, then fumbled for his wallet. He threw a handful of bills on the table, picked up the box she'd left behind, and followed her. He caught up to her in the parking lot. She was leaning against the car, looking down, her arms crossed. "What on earth is going on?" Jim said.

Sarah looked at him dully. "You didn't give me jewelry." Jim heard no accusation in her declaration, only sadness and betrayal.

Jim looked at her. "Well, maybe if you hadn't lit out so fast, you would have checked the card that came with the shoes."

"What?"

With a touch of annoyance, Jim repeated the words. When it registered, she took the box from him and looked inside. Off to the side of the shoes, a birthday card nestled. She opened the card and read the message: "Happy birthday to my special girl. Love, Jim. P.S. Check in the shoes." She took out one shoe and slid her hand inside. Nothing. She put the shoe back, picked up the other, and a sparkling amethyst bracelet slid into view. She gasped. "It's beautiful!"

His words were terse. "Yeah. Hope you like it."

She looked at him and saw the puzzled hurt that shown in his eyes. "Jim, I'm so sorry!"

He took a breath. "It was just meant as a little joke. Would you fill me in on what's happening here?"

She grimaced. "Well, I guess I have a few issues you don't know about. Some baggage from my youth. I never realized the extent of it or how much it's affected me. I'll tell you. I want to, but not in a parking lot."

He looked at her. "That's fine. What say we take a walk down The Grand Promenade?"

She smiled at him and took the hand Jim had offered her.

In the minutes that followed, Sarah told Jim things she'd never told anyone. Jim's jaw clenched as he imagined a much younger Sarah taking care of her mom, her voice quavering when she answered the phone and heard creditors on the other end. He could see her, worrying whether her mom would buy food or spend the little bit of money she had on alcohol.

"I knew your mom died before you finished high school," Jim said, "but the way you described her, she seemed like a saint."

"You can tell a story the way it is," Sarah said, "or you can tell it the way you want it to be."

The night seemed to be the perfect cover for telling secrets, and Sarah continued as they walked down the picturesque street. "She could surprise you. This one time, she picked me up early at school — I must have been twelve or so — and we went to a shop that had every kind of candy you can imagine.

"We got Sugar Babies and Hershey bars and these cherry suckers that were as big as biscuits. We got Coca-Colas and rode around all afternoon, playing the radio and eating candy.

"She did the best she could, Jim. At least she did on days like that."

An orange GTO passed by, its engine growling like a tiger. Jim had a desire to sweep Sarah up in his arms, to carry her like a child, to stop every bad thing she might face in the future.

Sarah pulled him forward, wanting to talk more, remembering her mom's advice to marry a man who would love her all the days of her life. Sarah was the same age now as her mom was then. She looked at her bracelet, one amethyst linked to another, that gleamed under the nearby street light. It all but sparkled, but it was not nearly as bright as Jim's devotion.

# CHAPTER 10 — A GAME FOR DORRIE

A pitiful whine made Jeb Compton look up from his copy of the *Hurlin Express.* His large bluetick coonhound sat on his butt on the porch and shook his head violently. Despite his best effort, a clawed creature stayed attached to one of the dog's long ears. Jeb dropped the papr, stood up, and went over to his hound.

"Dang it, Homer! You been down muckin' around the pond again and got a crawdad clamped on for your trouble. Hold still while I try to pry it off."

It took some doing, but finally the crawdad's claw released its grip. Homer looked at Jeb as if expecting a tongue lashing. Jeb patted Homer's head instead.

"I reckon you've paid a price for your nosing around. If you learnt something, there be no need for harsh words on my part. I'll put this little fella in a bucket and drop him back at the pond in a bit."

After depositing the crawdad, Jeb settled back in his white oak rocker and picked up the paper. He read awhile, then looked over at Homer. "It say here that The Roundup be celebrating being open for forty years. That's a good long time, but I reckon what they been serving ain't never going out of style."

The Roundup, established during the twenties as a speakeasy during Prohibition, stood as a landmark in Hurlin. It achieved local notoriety when visited by Alvin "Creepy" Karpis, leader of the Ma Barker Gang, as he passed through on his way to Hot Springs. Now, in the seventies, it still provided sustenance of all kinds: beer, smoked sausages, a jukebox filled with country records, two-stepping, and companionship. Its patrons ranged from good old boys to college students looking for some excitement. Drunken disputes erupted at times, but they were usually resolved in some fashion — a few by further discussion, others by fists, and the remainder by the six-foot, two-hundred-and-forty-pound bouncer. This night, however, presented a new method of resolution.

As the jukebox played, Conway Twitty's distinctive voice doled out "Hello Darlin'" to an appreciative crowd. Two men seated at a wooden table near the bar stared at each other. "Let's settle this at the pool table."

The speaker was Dan Carver, a thirty-two-year old barrel-chested man with a bushy red beard. Dan gripped the arms of the knotty pine chair. He stood unsteadily, pushed back his chair, and tugged up his belt, the big turquoise and silver buckle glinting in the light.

Billy Paxton's deep green eyes studied Dan for a few moments. After a pitcher of beer apiece, Billy was feeling no pain, but he could tell Dan was closer to hammered. He brushed back his mid-length brown hair, slid his lean, muscular frame from his chair, then joined Dan by the pool table.

"What's the game?"

Dan pondered. "How's about eight-ball?"

"Okay by me."

Like the men who selected it, the game was straightforward and uncomplicated. Each player had to sink seven balls — either the solid colors, numbered one through seven, or the striped colors, numbered nine through fifteen. When one man accomplished this, he could try for the black eight-ball. If he sank it before his opponent, he won. If an accident occurred, and the eight-ball dropped before its time, the player responsible lost. If his cue ball went in, he lost his turn.

Billy racked up the balls with tanned and work-roughened hands, arranging them in a triangle with the eight-ball in the middle. He took the break on a coin flip, cued up, and managed to pocket the maroon-striped fifteen-ball.

He glanced at Dan. "Looks like I've got stripes."

Dan snorted. "So's a zebra, but I never seen one worth a darn at pool."

Dan brayed at his own cleverness and looked over to the bar for approval. One of the patrons licked his forefinger and marked a one in the air. Dan liked that and looked even happier when Billy muffed his next shot and lost his turn.

Dan found his spot and took aim. "Now watch how it's done."

He sighted down his cue stick and gave the dull white cue

ball a vicious poke. Unfortunately, he hit it under center. The ball soared off the table, bounced twice on the worn oak floor, and landed in a potted cactus plant. The bar patrons erupted in laughter, quickly quelled by a fierce glare from Dan.

Billy strolled over to the cactus, retrieved the ball, and brushed the dirt off it. He sauntered back and placed the ball on the table. His lips twitched as he strove to maintain a deadpan expression.

"Heck of a shot."

If Dan felt embarrassed, you couldn't tell; the beer already had his face flushed to a rosy hue.

"Your turn," he muttered.

And so it went. Dan and Billy traded shots — verbally and otherwise. As the game progressed, it became evident that Billy's limited pool skill was nicely offset by Dan's lack of coordination. The game showed no sign of finishing anytime soon. Especially since Dan had gotten distracted by a barmaid's impressive cleavage when she bent to wipe off a table just to the right of the pool table.

"Come on, Dan. Concentrate."

Dan reluctantly brought his eyes back to the game. He managed to sink the orange-striped thirteen ball. "Dang fine shot if I do say so myself."

Billy whistled. "It's probably the best shot you've made all night. Dadgum shame, though."

Dan blinked. "What do you mean?"

A smile played on Billy's lips. "Well, you done sank one of my balls." When that information sank in, Dan cursed and ran his fingers through his thick, red hair. Then he wobbled over to the bar.

"Hey, Sam," Dan said as he pointed toward the men's room. "I got to go see a man about a horse. Keep an eye on Billy while I'm gone. See that he don't mess with the table?"

Sam Barstow, the town's lawyer, assured Dan he would, and Dan headed off unsteadily while Sam ambled over to speak to Billy.

Nodding to Sam, Billy slapped his knee, "Dan looks as surefooted as a pig on stilts, don't he?"

"Yeah, I just hope his aim is better in there than it is out here. Say, what are you two arguing about this time?"

Billy grinned. "The usual — which one of us is going to talk Dorrie in to marrying him."

Sam raised his eyebrows. "And you're settling it with a game of pool? Does Dorrie have any idea what's going on here?"

Billy shrugged. "Seems like Dorrie can't make up her mind. Me and Dan figure it's up to us to decide who backs off."

"And you think she'll go along with that?"

Billy laughed. "Heck, she'll probably thank us."

Sam shook his head. "Playing a game of pool for the hand of a lady. Sounds kinda disrespectful to me."

"Come on, Sam. You know me and Dan; we been best friends since elementary school. Ain't no way we going to risk that by brawling over a woman, even one as fine as Dorrie."

Dan reappeared at the table. "All right then, let's get to it."

"Buddy, you might want to zip your fly first."

Dan laughed and zipped his pants in front of God and everybody.

Billy had one ball left to sink before he could try for the eight. Dan had only the eight left to shoot for, but it was Billy's turn. He sighed, leaned over to aim, and stroked the cue ball. Banking off the side rail, it tapped the eleven toward the corner pocket. He sucked in his breath as the ball hung on the edge before dropping in.

Dan slapped his forehead. "Dang! You got a straight shot at the eight." Dan staggered as he moved back from the pool table. "I'm going to miss Dorrie. I might even miss your old hide ever now and again."

"What are you jawing about? We ain't gonna be going nowhere."

"No, but you'll be married and all. That changes ever last thing."

Billy scratched his head. "Well, Dan, won't we be in the same pickle if I miss the shot and you win?"

Dan frowned. "You know, Billy, I can't think worth a darn in here." He rubbed his forehead. "Too much noise."

Billy seemed to consider this. "That juke box is louder than them stock car races down by the levy."

Dan cupped his hand around his ear as if he couldn't hear. "And the Peevy brothers is shouting over there at the bar. Act like they was raised in a dadgum barn."

"Ain't it the truth?" Billy asked. "Besides, old Sam here thinks we ain't being respectful to Dorrie."

"We was raised a heap better than that. We'd never disrespect no lady, let alone our Dorrie."

"Dang straight," Billy said, and then he slung his arm around Dan's shoulders, and they headed back to the bar.

After Dan and Billy left, Sam peered at the table. He considered the two balls resting on the crisp, green felt. He was thinking that, unlike those balls, few things in life are clearly black or white.

# CHAPTER 11 — THREE KINDS OF RAIN

In response to a mournful howl, Jeb Compton, barefoot and shirt halfway buttoned, barged out the front door and onto his porch. He stopped abruptly and stared at the spectacle in front of him. "Dang it, Homer. How in the name of all that's holy did you get your head stuck in that wash bucket?"

Jeb gripped the sides of the bucket, gritted his teeth, and yanked, but the bucket remained firmly in place. A heavy round of tugging, grunting, and yelping commenced before Homer's large head popped free. Homer plopped back on his butt, and Jeb staggered back a few steps. "I swear, Homer."

He stopped short. Homer stood with head bowed, tail tucked, and a woebegone look on his face. Jeb reached down and ruffled the furry head. "It's okay, boy. I reckon I done my share of stupid in my day. It's about time for breakfast, don't you think?"

Homer barked his agreement, and Jeb went back in the house to finish dressing and to fix their meals. After eating, Jeb assumed his usual spot on the porch chair and leafed through *The Hurlin Express.* "Hey, Homer. It say here Sally Fenton — you know, Nora's girl — got one of them intern positions at a news station in Little Rock. Nora told me Sally graduated from that community college she were attending, so I guess it's time for her to go out and make her mark. She's a feisty one, that Sally. Smart, too. I wonder how she'll like it."

Sally Fenton tucked a loose strand of blonde hair behind her ear, pushed her wire-rimmed glasses up on her nose, and blew out a breath. This is going to take some getting used to, she thought, as she listened to the police scanner, hoping to hear a bank robbery underway or the arrest of someone important. Since she landed the job as news assistant, she'd written only two stories for the six o'clock newscast, one about a woman turning one hundred, and another about an uptick in barge traffic on the Arkansas River. She thought she'd done a great job, but then the show's producer called her over to point out a series of mistakes.

Other than that, she'd answered the phones that seemed to ring non-stop, handing off news tips to the assignment editor. Sally thought working in a newsroom would be exciting. That's why she'd studied broadcast journalism. And now she was learning that there was a whole lot they didn't cover in her classes. Still, she couldn't think of one place she'd rather be.

Skip Banyon, the weatherman for television station KATV, finished his forecast, strolled over to Sally's desk, and blessed her with a pearly-white smile. "Ah, Miss Fenton, working hard, I see. Very commendable."

"Oh, hello, Mr. Banyon. Can I help you?" she asked, one ear still trained on the scanner.

"I was wondering if you had any plans for the evening. There's a good steak restaurant inside Union Station I've been wanting to try."

Sally hesitated. Edna, the secretary for the news director, had confided that she found Skip Banyon a bit of a bore and somewhat full of himself, but men hadn't exactly been beating down Sally's door lately. Maybe Edna's misjudged him, she thought.

"Sure, Mr. Banyon. Sounds like fun."

"Excellent. I'll pick you up at seven." He flashed her that famous smile again. "And call me Skip," he said.

Sally adjusted her glasses again, a nervous habit she'd had since grade school. "Do you know where I live?" Skip merely winked and disappeared down the hall.

After work, Sally walked the four blocks to her apartment building. She climbed two flights of worn stairs, careful to avoid the gum, cigarette butts, and food wrappers she encountered, then unlocked the door to her apartment.

Once inside, Sally surveyed her domain. One dresser with cigarette burns on top and two handles missing from the drawers. One single bed with sagging springs and lumpy mattress. One lamp with a frayed cord wrapped in electrical tape and peeling plastic on the shade.

Enough, she thought. At least there aren't any roaches. She looked around, wondering how Skip Banyon would see her place and decided not to find out. She'd get ready and wait for him in front of the building.

Skip met her there at 7:30 p.m. He wore a smart blue blazer, flashy red tie, and perfectly parted hair. "My apologies for being late, Miss Fenton. They needed me at the station to check out the new isobar readings, and it took a bit longer than I anticipated."

Sally crossed her arms. He hadn't even bothered to call. She looked him over for a second and decided to let it go. It wasn't a hill to die on.

"I guess a weatherman is on call a lot."

He sniffed. "The term is meteorologist. And yes, I'm always on call."

Skip pointed to her apartment building just behind them. "You might want to go get an umbrella. Indications are there will be some precipitation."

"You think it's going to rain?"

"I believe I just said that."

Sally felt heat beginning to rise in her cheeks. "No, you said 'precipitation.' As a meteorologist — she enunciated each syllable — you surely know that precipitation also includes snow, sleet, and hail."

His ears reddened. "Of course, I do. But umbrellas are needed primarily for rain."

Sally clenched her fists. "Okay, then. I'll run get my umbrella, and we'll go." She turned to step back into the building, and he was right behind her. "You," she said, pointing a finger, "you wait here."

When she returned, they walked to the building's parking lot where he steered her toward a flashy British racing-green Porsche 911 convertible.

Sally whistled. "You meteorologists must do pretty well for yourselves."

Skip shrugged. "It's not that big a deal. It had sixty thousand miles on it when I got it, so it cost me half what a new one goes for."

"Still, it's a Porsche."

"Yes, indeed, and because of that, it's in the shop as much as it's on the road."

"Then why did you get it?"

It took Skip a few seconds to speak. "I got it for my image."

"Your image?"

"Yes. 'Local celebrity lives large.' That sort of thing."

Before she could stop herself, Sally said, "Celebrity? You?"

Skip raised an eyebrow. "Haven't you seen my picture on the billboards?"

Sally burst out laughing. When she could draw a breath, she said, "Do you ever listen to yourself?"

She braced for an explosion, but none came. She looked up at Skip and saw a smile.

"Truthfully, I try not to. I usually sound like an ass. Let me get your door."

Sally slid onto the plush leather passenger seat, feeling totally confused. Drops of rain fell, fogging Sally's glasses, and Skip put the top up. The rain intensified minute by minute, and soon the car's headlights were penetrating only ten feet ahead. The windshield wipers struggled to clear the rain as it drummed down. "Not ideal driving conditions," Skip said. "Mind if we pull over to the curb for a while and see if it slacks off?"

"That sounds like a good idea."

As they waited, Sally wondered what to say. "What kind of rain would you call this?" she asked after a bit, speaking as loudly as she could over the sound of the downpour.

Skip drummed his fingers on the steering wheel. "There are only three categories of rain, of course," he nearly shouted. "There's convectional rain which occurs in regions that are hot and wet, relief rain which usually occurs in coastal areas, and frontal rain which occurs when a cold front meets a warm front. Due to our location, and what the isobars showed me, I'm opting for the third."

Sally's rolled her eyes. This is too much, she thought. "You certainly do seem to know your weather."

Skip smiled. "I strive to be accurate."

"But, don't you think it's silly to limit rain to three kinds?"

"What do you mean?"

"Three is boring, especially when you put them in those stuffy terms."

Skip's raised his eyebrows. "And how would you classify them?"

"Well, first, there's fine rain. Back in my hometown of Hurlin, we'd call that misting, or spitting, or spotting, or piddling. When it comes down a little harder, it's sprinkling, or drizzling, or pattering. A strong rain is raining cats and dogs or bucket loads. Even stronger is a downpour, or drumming, or pelting, or a gutter washer, or a frog strangler. And when all hell breaks loose, it's a gully washer or a tree floater." She cleared her throat and switched to what she thought of as a professorial lecture tone. "All things considered I'd say this one qualifies as a gutter washer."

Skip stared at Sally like he'd stepped on a rake that reared up and smacked him in the face. "Miss Fenton, that is the most incredible litany I have ever heard."

Sally grinned, and her dimples showed. "Well, Mr. Banyon — I mean Skip — the night's still young."

Skip drove to Union Station on West Markham. He parked, and they entered the lower level where they found the Tracks Inn LTD, the most talked-about restaurant in that part of town. Sally gasped when she saw the prices. Skip, however, seemed unconcerned and ordered a Delmonico steak, a bottle of Zinfandel and two glasses. Sally chose six-inch sirloin, and during the meal, which Sally found incredible, she noticed several diners glancing in their direction and whispering.

"Some of those people keep looking over here," she said.

Skip looked around the room, smiling and nodding. "You get accustomed to it," he said and straightened his tie. "More wine?"

Sally frowned. "Back to the celebrity thing. You seem to have a rather high opinion of yourself, Mr. Banyon."

Skip shrugged. "I thought we agreed that you'd call me Skip. Anyway, it is what it is."

Sally bit back a retort. Instead, she said, "It's a wonderful meal, and I thank you for it, but it's getting kind of late, and I'm working dayside tomorrow."

Skip looked disappointed, but he nodded. "Very well, then. Let's get you home."

# CHAPTER 12 — SECOND CHANCES

Sally Fenton was making beat calls, ringing every sheriff, police department, and fire department in KATV's viewing area, seeing what crime or disaster might have happened in the last few hours. It's how every day started, and she'd gotten so close to a few dispatchers who took her calls, she felt like they were friends. When she hung up from her final call, the news director's secretary — and Sally's friend — was standing in front of her.

"Edna, where did you come from?"

Edna grinned. "I'm assuming you're not asking for a biology lesson. I thought I'd check on you. Are you doing okay?"

Sally propped her elbow on the desk and put her chin in her hand. "I'm trying as hard as I can, but there's so much to learn. And nobody has the time to teach me much of anything! Everybody's running around like jackrabbits."

"That's the news business, Sally. It's like juggling cats, I swear."

"It's exactly like that." Sally looked at her watch. "It's about a minute until my coffee break. That is if the world doesn't collapse in the next sixty seconds."

Edna nodded. "Mind if I join you? There's something I've been dying to ask you."

They went to the break room, and each selected a ceramic mug with a KATV logo. Sally poured a cup of coffee, blew on it a few times, took a sip and grimaced. "This stuff is really bad."

"Yep," Edna said. "The maintenance man told me they use any leftovers to unclog the drains."

Sally laughed. "You are so funny. So, what did you want to ask?"

Edna walked to the door and closed it. "How was your date with Mr. Wonderful last night?"

"You know, I'm honestly not sure what to make of him. That man is a giant ball of contradictions. One minute, he's being a pompous ass, and the next, he's a sweetheart."

Edna's eyes sparkled. "So, give me some details."

"Sorry, you're going to have to take a rain check on that. I've been away from the scanners too long already."

"Okay, but I'm going to hold you to it."

Sally returned to her desk and started looking through a stack of local papers, making sure the KATV news team hadn't missed a big story somehow. She didn't notice Skip Banyon's arrival until he cleared his throat. When she looked up, he beamed his hundred-watt smile. "Miss Fenton. How are we doing today?"

Sally leveled her gaze at him. "I can't speak for 'we,' but I'm passable."

Skip's smile faltered a bit, but he continued. "I really enjoyed myself last night, and I'd love to see you again. You have a rather refreshing outlook on things."

"Must be because I'm just a small-town girl. I haven't learned the art of being big city yet, and I probably never will."

Skip's smile was just a trace of its former glory. "Did I do something to offend you?"

She frowned. "Not specifically, no. But trying to figure you out gives me a headache."

Skip's eyebrows raised. "Are you saying that you don't want to go out with me again?"

"We're too different. I hope that doesn't put a dent in your celebrity psyche."

A crease appeared in Skip's forehead, and his mouth turned down at the corners. "I must say that's a bit harsh, Sally, and not entirely fair, but if that's how you feel —" He looked as if he had something to say, decided against it. He spun on his heels and swiftly departed.

Sally blew out the breath she hadn't realized she'd been holding and shook her head. She could have been nicer, she realized, but something about Skip Banyon made her emotions rise to the surface.

The rest of the workday dragged to its completion. After checking her purse, Sally stopped at a nearby Kroger store and bought a can of Spam, a few slices of American cheese, a loaf of Wonder bread, and a jar of Miracle Whip. She thought back to that wonderful meal she'd had last night and sighed. The total bill at the store didn't even match the price of one of those steaks.

When she reached her apartment, she looked around. Her meager belongings continued to make her sad. What she wouldn't give for a beer at that moment, but beer was a luxury that wasn't in her budget. That was the thing about working in news. It sounded glamorous, but the pay was abysmal, at least until you rose to the top. Like Skip Banyon had done, she thought. She sighed, made a Spam sandwich and a promise not to think of Skip anymore tonight.

The next day, she arrived at work and found a vase of Shasta daisies sitting on a corner of her desk. Surprised, she read the card: *I hope you'll give me a chance to make amends. If so, I'll pick you up at seven.* Skip's name was etched beneath. She sniffed the fresh linen scent of the blooms, shook her head, and got back to work.

During lunch, she opted for McDonald's, a treat she really couldn't afford. She loved the place, though, with its Mansard roof, utilitarian design, and the scent of french fries that made her feel happy for no particular reason. She waited while her order was filled, then selected a booth. Edna popped up and put her tray down. "Fancy meeting you here."

Sally smiled. "I decided to treat myself today."

"Good for you. So, about that date?"

Sally shook her head. "You don't give up, do you?"

Edna grinned. "You better believe it. Now, spill the beans."

Between munching on her french fries and cheeseburger, Sally filled Edna in on what had transpired.

Edna's eyes widened in disbelief. "So, after he took you to that expensive restaurant, you turned him down for another date? And he still sent flowers and asked you out again?" Edna shook her head. "Honey, you're something else."

"Hey, I'm not the bad guy here. I can't help it if he rubs me the wrong way. We just don't have anything in common, and his self-importance really irritates me."

Edna raised her eyebrows. "Well, it's your business, but do you think you've really given the guy a chance?"

Sally frowned. "Weren't you the one who thought he was

full of himself?"

"Honey, he's a man on television. They're all that way. They go out to eat, and someone notices them. They show up at a high school football game, and someone wants their autograph. Everyone thinks they're far-out. After a while, they do too."

"That doesn't show much character," Sally said. "Look, let's just drop the subject and finish eating." Edna nodded, stung by Sally's words, and the rest of the meal passed in an uncomfortable silence.

After work, Sally walked to her apartment, where she soon found herself sitting on the edge of her bed. Flopping backward, she stared at the ceiling. She thought back on her conversation with Edna and tried to decide what to do. The daisies made her decision for her. At 6:00 p.m., she started getting ready, and 7:00 p.m. found her waiting on the sidewalk in front of her apartment.

Skip walked up a minute later, and Sally tried not to gawk at the transformation she witnessed. Skip's hair was clean but tousled, his blue chambray shirt was untucked over a pair of Levi blue jeans, and his feet were clad in a pair of Adidas sneakers. He gave a tentative smile. "Didn't know if you'd be here. Are you ready to go eat?" All she could do was nod.

They walked to the parking lot, and he indicated their ride — a red '68 Chevy truck. After opening her door, he got in. "I thought we'd go to my favorite place. I hope you like it."

After driving a few blocks, Skip turned onto Markham. About ten minutes later, he pulled the truck into the Minute Man parking lot. "They have the best burgers. Is it okay with you if we eat in the truck?"

Sally again nodded and fidgeted with her glasses. Skip went to the carry-out window and returned shortly with two Big M burgers, fries, and Cokes. As they were eating, Skip asked. "How do you like it?"

"It's really good, but —"

Skip grinned. "But what?"

Sally stared at him. "Who are you? You don't seem anything like the Skip Banyon I went out with last night."

Skip laughed. "I'm just me. The me I don't usually show to people around here."

Sally shook he head. "You are seriously messing with my mind, here. If this is the real you, then why the charade?"

Skip seemed to consider his answer. "Because in this business, image is everything, and I try to provide the people what they want and expect. I busted my tail to get where I am, and that's the truth. Most people seem to be happy with the result, but I could tell you weren't one of them. I like that about you, I do. So, I asked for another try, hoping it wasn't too late."

Sally concentrated on her food, which gave her time to think. When she'd consumed the last fry, she looked at him. "Well, you certainly had me fooled, and I really thought I was done with you, but I'm glad you made one mistake."

Skip frowned. "A mistake? What do you mean?"

"The flowers."

Skip looked puzzled. "The daisies? You didn't like them?"

Sally smiled. "I loved them. It's just what this country girl would want to see on her desk."

Skip scratched his head. "I'm not sure I'm following."

Sally reached over and took his hand. "If it had been roses, which is what your Skip Banyon, big-time meteorologist, would have sent, I wouldn't be here right now. But it was daisies, and that gave me hope."

Skip looked down at her hand, then up at her face. "Well, if that's the case, then thank the good Lord for mistakes."

# CHAPTER 13 — THE RATING GAME

Sitting on the porch in his white oak rocker, Jeb Compton took a swallow from his morning bottle of Coors, something he did every morning he worked in his soybean field. As was his habit, he thumbed through the pages of the *Hurlin Express.*

"Hey, Homer, it say in them want ads that Drucks, that food company that delivers right to your door, is hiring for one of them taste tester positions."

Homer, Jeb's big bluetick hound, hunkered down in the tall field grass behind the garden, not far from where Jeb sat. He had staked out a spot near a groundhog burrow and waited with rapt attention for an appearance. Distracted when Jeb addressed him, he looked away at just the wrong moment. A furry, brown head popped out of the hole, spied Homer, and beat a hasty retreat. Homer, no doubt dejected, hung his head. "You know, I always thought that there would be a dream job. Trying all kinds of food and drinks and getting paid for it. Problem is, them taste buds of mine ain't that keen. But for folks as has got the ability, it could be right nice. You know, I think I'll give Bertie Mae a call. She's always winning them blue ribbons at the fair for her baking. This here testing might be right down her alley."

An old adage states that ladies don't sweat — they glisten. By the time Bertie May Johnson had hoed in her garden for fifteen minutes under the unforgiving Arkansas sun, she had glistened about a quart. Certain Hurlin residents might have made unkind remarks about that. They might have smugly observed that her excessive weight no doubt contributed. Unfortunately, if the situation had been reversed, Bertie would have done the same. She could be the bigger person, it seemed, in size only.

Mopping her brow with a large handkerchief, she resumed attacking the weeds sprouting up around the corn. The heat, weeds, and gophers made her wonder about the worth of her efforts, but thoughts of ripe, juicy kernels of corn, slathered in butter and well-salted, sustained her. After another fifteen minutes, she heard the telephone ring. She propped the hoe against an elm tree and headed for the house to answer it.

"Hello."

"Howdy, Bertie. This be Jeb Compton. How you doing?"

"Well, I was busy hoeing, but you interrupted that."

"Sorry 'bout that. I won't keep you. I just wanted to see if you knowed about that taste testing ad in the paper."

Her voice grew harsh. "Is that supposed to be some kind of joke about my weight? Because if it is —"

Alarm bells went off in Jeb's head. "Whoa now, Bertie. It weren't no such. I seen this ad in today's paper. Said that Drucks over in Richland is hiring taste testers for some of their products. Since you're a mighty fine cook, I figured it might interest you. That's all."

Bertie's voice calmed a bit. "Well, okay then. What else did the ad say?"

"Not too much. Just give the address and phone number and said to hurry on over to their place to fill out a application. I can give you them details if you want."

"All right. Let me get a pencil."

Bertie got paper and pencil from the catch-all drawer in her kitchen and wrote down the information. She gruffly thanked Jeb, said goodbye, got a glass of sweet tea from the refrigerator, and went to sit on the sofa under the ceiling fan.

While she cooled off, she turned things over in her mind. Bertie knew she'd been prickly with Jeb, but she'd been the butt of so many jokes about her weight, she immediately went on the offensive. Bertie closed her eyes, remembering how hard she'd worked to keep her figure, sometimes waking up and going to bed hungry, and how she thought how she looked was the key to keeping her husband happy.

Apparently not, since Clarence high-tailed it out of town with his secretary, a curvy redhead fifteen years younger than Bertie. That first week after he left, Bertie ate almost nothing. But the next week, lying in her bed surrounded by soggy tissues, she ate a big bag of Fritos. The salty corn chips filled her up the way her marriage never had. In a month, she'd outgrown all her clothes. In six months, she'd become the talk of the town, instead of her no-good husband, a fact she's still sore about.

Well, Bertie thought, I'm going to get this weight off one of these days. But right now, I'm going to clean up and go see what that ad is all about. Lord knows I could use the money.

Bertie drove the twenty miles to Richland and parked her '73 green Rambler in the Drucks' parking lot. Once inside, a slim young brunette approached her. Bertie hated her on sight.

"May I help you?"

"I'm here to see about that taste testing thing. What do I need to do?"

"Well, you need to fill out an application, and then we'll administer a screening test for sensory ability."

"Say what, now?"

"You'll be asked to identify different tastes: salty, bitter, sweet, sour."

"That sounds easy enough."

"Well, the concentrations are quite low. Some folks can't do it."

Bertie smiled. "Won't be a problem. What else?"

"You have to smell containers with different flavors and identify them."

"I can do that."

"You can't be colorblind either, which is more of a problem for men than women, but we still check."

Bertie stared at her. "Why on earth does that matter?"

"Well, the visual aspect of food is important as well as the taste and smell."

"Oh. I get that. I'm not colorblind. Anything else?"

"Let's see. Oh, yes, and you can't have any food allergies."

Bertie glared at her. "Do I *look* like I have any food allergies?"

The brunette wisely chose not to comment and handed Bertie the application. After she filled it out and handed it back, Bertie was led to a small room with a table and several folding chairs. On the table, she saw two racks of vials containing liquids. She carefully seated herself and looked at the brunette.

"Please sample the vials in the rack nearest you. Taste each one, left to right, and tell me what you taste."

Bertie tilted each to her tongue for a moment and set it back in the rack. She smiled.

"Sour, bitter, salty, sweet."

"Excellent. Now sample the vials in the other rack by smell, again left to right, and tell me what flavor each is."

Bertie copied her motions from the first trial, only sniffing instead of tasting. "Ginger, saffron, cinnamon, vanilla."

"Impressive."

"Nah, it was easy-peasy. So, do I qualify?"

"You most certainly do. The product testing will be in two days, starting at 9:00 a.m. There will be several other testers working as well."

"Fine by me."

"Then we'll see you Thursday."

When Thursday rolled around, Bertie drove to the plant and was ushered into a room with five other women. They all sat on one side of a long table that was piled with samples. Bertie pulled out a chair and sat down. A minute later, a short, balding man with glasses and a white lab coat entered.

He looked around the room and smiled. "Good day, ladies. I'm Jim Thornton. I will be administering the tests. We have a new product today: Vanilla Bean Chocolate Cake." Bertie smiled widely. Could it get any better?

"Here at Drucks, we do organoleptic testing to ensure that the food is appealing to consumers and that it keeps batch-to-batch consistency. Now then, you will be taking a small bite of the cake and evaluate each ingredient by rating the taste attributes. Does it taste buttery? Can you taste the vanilla? How intense is the flavor? How does it feel in your mouth? Did it crumble or melt? That sort of thing."

Bertie's smile lessened considerably.

"There can be as many as thirty attributes on the form that I will provide you. You will rate each attribute on a scale of one to ten. In the days to come, we will test the same product many times, and your scores will then be compared to your previous scores. You will get individual reports on your consistency."

Bertie's smile had gone the way of the passenger pigeon. Jim smiled. "Are you all ready? Let's begin. We should be done in a couple of hours."

Bertie grimaced into the handset of her phone. "I tell you, Clara, it was brutal. It was: take a bite, chew it up, roll it around on your tongue, then grab the form and commence rating. Over, and over, and over again. By the time we finished, my taste buds were going numb.

"No. You weren't allowed to swallow. You had to spit it out! I'd eaten most of the first piece before I found out that little tidbit. It was mighty embarrassing, I can tell you.

"No. It wasn't even that good. I guess those factories can't compete with homemade.

"Will I go back? I don't know. On the one hand, the money's nice. On the other, well, I never thought I'd turn my nose up at food, but if I can't even eat it, what's the point?"

In the weeks that followed, Bertie found that her new job held some unexpected benefits. The abundance of food, offered in small bites she wasn't allowed to swallow, taught her discipline. At home, she began cutting her portions in two. By the fall, she was down seven pounds, and by Christmas, thirteen. She sometimes stood before the Fritos display down at the market, remembering how the weight of the chips on her tongue soothed all that emptiness after Clarence walked out. The chips soothed her, for sure, but now she isn't sure that she ever really tasted them at all.

## CHAPTER 14 — ROLE MODEL

"Dang it, Homer. Why'd you feel the need to go messing with a skunk? You smell worse than that old possum carcass you brung home last week."

Homer, the picture of abject misery, hung his big head so low that the hound's long ears dragged the ground. He gave a pitiful whine. Jeb left off his griping. "I know it ain't no picnic for you neither. Let's go see if we got the stuff to better the situation."

After he tied Homer to a porch post, Jeb hunted through the kitchen cabinets until he found what he needed. He measured out a fourth-cup baking soda, two teaspoons of dishwashing soap, a quart of hydrogen peroxide, and a quart of water, and dumped them in a pail. The mixture started fizzing. He added a wash cloth, grabbed some old towels, and went outside. Half-an-hour later, Jeb finished up and Homer smelled tolerable.

Jeb untied him and patted his hound. "I hope you learnt something from this, Homer. Sometimes, something that seems like a good idea at the time can turn out to stir up a hornet's nest."

Tommy Jenkins stumbled into the kitchen, trying not to trip over long johns that were two sizes too big. John Denver's catchy "Take Me Home, Country Roads" played over the Philco radio on the counter, and the red curls on Tommy's head bounced around as though keeping time to the beat.

His mother, stirring a bowl of pancake batter, looked up and smiled. "Morning, sleepyhead. How are you this fine day?"

Tommy made it to the yellow Formica kitchen table, pulled out a chair, and plopped down. He looked hopefully at his mother and asked for coffee.

Martha Jenkins set the bowl down on the counter, wiped her hands on her apron, and turned to face him. "Not today, young man. Maybe in a few years."

"Aw, Ma, I'm nine years old. Uncle Charlie said he started drinking it when he turned seven."

"Mayhap he did, and look how he turned out."

Tommy's face held a puzzled look. "What do you mean?"

His mother sucked in her breath as she realized what she'd said. "Oh, nothing. I'm just about ready to put some hotcakes on. Why don't you go get dressed, and they'll be ready when you get back."

Tommy headed to his room. "And mind you don't

lollygag. You got to catch the school bus in a bit, and Mr. Dooly's got a schedule to keep."

Tommy sighed. "I know, Ma."

After Tommy polished off a stack of three large cakes, he gathered up his school things, kissed his mama on the cheek, and headed down their country lane to catch the bus. Martha watched him till he disappeared from sight. He's a great kid, she thought. Growing up too fast. I wish his daddy could see him now. Jim would be so proud of him.

Her blue eyes teared up, and she wiped the tears away with her apron. It had been a hard two years since Jim had died in a backhoe accident, but they'd made it this far. Between her cashier's job at Winn-Dixie and selling eggs from their chicken house, she'd managed to make ends meet.

Martha went back in the kitchen and took a coffee mug from the cabinet. She spooned out a measure of freeze-dried coffee, poured hot water from the tea kettle over it, and stirred. Taking her mug to the table, she pulled out a chair and sat down. She took a sip and grimaced. The instant coffee didn't taste like the real thing at all.

Martha took another sip and put the cup down. She was feeling guilty, truth be told. Tommy adored his Uncle Charlie, her late husband's brother, and she'd talked bad about him. Jim and Charlie, she mused. Jim had been the silent type with not much to say; Charlie could talk the bark off a tree. Jim had been steady and dependable; Charlie showed up when not expected and came late when he was. Jim was tall, wiry, and well-groomed; Charlie had the start of a beer gut, and his beard stood in constant need of trimming. Jim was a straight arrow; Charlie, a pinball game. One thing they had both shared, though, was their love for Tommy.

She took a swallow of coffee and made a face. How long was I wool-gathering? she wondered. Martha rose from the table, heading for the hen house to collect eggs, and started getting ready for her shift at the Winn-Dixie.

Martha worked the register and tried to put a dent in the never-ending line of customers. Mabel, a coworker, came up to her. "Martha, the boss says you've got a telephone call."

"Did he say who it is?"

"Yeah, it's the school."

Alarm flashed on Martha's face. "Mabel, can you take over?"

"Sure, Hon, I got you covered."

Martha climbed the stairs leading to the office two at a time, knocked once on the door, and entered. The boss gestured toward the phone on his desk, then tapped his watch with an index finger. The meaning was unmistakable.

She lifted the handset to her ear. "Hello."

"Mrs. Jenkins?"

"Is Tommy okay?"

"Well, he was reported absent from his last period class, and we're checking to see if you know anything about that."

Martha's face turned pale. "I do not!"

"I see. Well, let's not worry just yet. We'd check with his bus driver, but they've already started their routes. I was wondering, would it be possible for you to be there when Tommy's bus arrives?"

"Yes, of course."

"Try not to worry. He probably just skipped class."

"He wouldn't do that. Not Tommy."

Martha hung up the receiver. "Boss," she said, "I've got to go."

He arched his eyebrows. "You've still got half-an-hour left on your shift."

"You'll just have to deal with that."

She all but ran to the parking lot where her old Ford waited.

Martha picked up the handset of her kitchen phone and dialed Charlie's number. When he answered, she told him that Tommy was missing. "You stay put, Martha. I'll be right over."

Ten minutes passed, and Charlie knocked on the door. As Martha filled him in, he glanced at the kitchen clock. "It's almost time for the bus to get here. Hop in my truck, and we'll wait at the end of your lane. If he's not on the bus, we'll go from there."

In a few minutes, the bus came into view. Martha sucked in her breath and put a death grip on Charlie's arm. The bus stopped, and Tommy got off. Martha, crying now, ran over, wrapped her arms around him and held tight. "Thank you, God. Thank you."

Tommy struggled in her arms. "Ma, it's hard to breathe."

She let go and took a step back. "Where were you last period? Did you skip class?"

His face fell, and she knew he was guilty. Anger overtook Martha, and before she knew it, she'd slapped him. "Don't you ever scare me like that again!"

Charlie, standing beside her, laid a hand on her arm. "Now, Martha."

She knocked his arm away. "Don't you dare! This is your fault for filling his head with all those stunts you pulled when you were his age. Take us down to the house."

Charlie looked as though she had slapped him, too, but he did as she said. When they were in the kitchen, she told them to sit down. She glared at Charlie. "I'll be lucky to have a job tomorrow, and I've got to call the school, but first I'm going to take a walk and try to cool down. You stay here with Tommy and figure out how to make things right. And I'm warning you, Charlie, no filling his head with your hairbrained stories."

Charlie looked at Tommy. "Well, boy, it looks like we both put our foot in it this time."

Tommy sat and rubbed his cheek. "I never seen her so mad, Uncle Charlie. I just cut the one class. You told me you used to do stuff like that all the time."

"Yeah, son, I done a lot of foolhardy things. That don't make 'em right. I guess I was trying to make you think I was someone to look up to." He sighed. "But I ain't nothing special. Do you know why your ma's so upset?"

Tommy thought it over. "Because," he started, and his head dropped. "Because, I reckon with Pa gone, I'm all she's got."

"That's right — in her mind, anyway. She's scared to death of losing you, too. So, here's what I think needs doing. We both got to grow up a little bit. Apologize to her and really mean it. And no more knuckleheaded stunts." Just then, Charlie and Tommy heard footsteps on the porch, just outside the kitchen. As Martha turned the doorknob, they stood and prepared to face the music.

Martha looked them over, hands on her hips. "Charlie," she said, "Thanks for your help today, and apologies if I hurt your feelings. But let me say this, I won't let anybody around Tommy who might lead him astray, and that includes you. Jim was mighty fond of you, and he asked me there at the end to lean on you after he was gone."

Tommy stood to leave. "Sit down," Martha said. "You need to hear this."

"Just this morning, I was thinking I'd been too hard on you, Charlie, and then Tommy goes and tries to act just like you.

"Tomorrow, Tommy is going to apologize to his teacher and his principal. And he's grounded for a month.

"I got no way to discipline you, Charlie Jenkins, but I can keep you away from here. So, for a month, don't show your face, don't pick up the phone and call.

"I'll talk to you after that, and we'll see if there's a way to fix this."

Charlie eyes watered, and he cleared his throat. Tommy tried to step in, saying, "Uncle Charlie was giving me what-for about today!" but Charlie held his hand up, signaling him to stop.

Charlie ruffled Tommy's hair and headed for the door. "We'll both do better," he said to Martha, his voice croaking as he spoke. "I promise you on everything I ever loved."

Martha felt her resolve waning, so she looked away. "We'll talk in a month," she said. "We'll see what we can do."

Martha watched Charlie walk to his truck. She looked at Tommy, who had his father's eyes and his uncle's thirst for adventure. What she wouldn't give to have her Jim back. What she wouldn't give to ask him what to do.

Tommy wrapped his arms around her, and she let the boy sink into her. She had a few hard years ahead of her, the kind where you have to sleep with one eye open. She'd keep an eagle eye on her boy. She only hoped it would be enough.

## CHAPTER 15 — HOT CHOPS AND COLD TRUTH

As they trudged along the road's shoulder, Jeb looked down at his hound. "Homer, I've had better days. First, my old John Deere tractor won't start, and it took two hours of fussing and cussing to get her up and running. Next, I find that new herbicide I doused on them soybeans a while back ain't living up to its billing. Then, I got to tote you to the vet for what turns out to be a case of garbage gut. And finally, we get run off the road and stuck in the ditch cause that Bagwell kid be driving too fast and slewing around.

"And did that no-account pecker-head stop to help us out? No. He just waved and kept on going. Now we're having to trek over to Luke Taylor's to ask him to pull us out. That Bagwell kid is a heap of trouble, Homer, and I'm of a mind to go have a talk with his folks."

Eyes wild and cheeks flushed, Ma stormed out of the kitchen waving a potato masher like a band director's baton. Flecks of potatoes flew in all directions. "Where is that boy? Them pork chops is getting cold. If he don't get here soon, I'm going to jerk him up and twist a knot in his tail."

Seated at the faded yellow Formica table with her family, Karen Bagwell's green eyes squinted behind her glasses, and her mouth pulled down in a frown. Yeah, right, she thought. Like anything will happen to the golden boy.

Her father, seated in his red long-johns, spoke up. "Now Mollie, don't be getting in a lather. I'm sure he'll be here soon."

Granny, sitting in her gingham housedress, nodded. She might be agreeing with Pa, Karen thought, or she might be keeping time to a tune in her head that only she could hear. With Granny, you never knew. At least she was wearing something. She'd been known to show up for dinner in the altogether which caused a loss of appetite for anyone present.

Ma snorted. "Well, he'd better be here soon if he knows what's good for him."

Bull-pucky, Karen thought. Most likely he was out raising Billy Ned somewhere and forgot all about the time. When he did drag in, he'd have some lame excuse ready, and it would do the trick. It always did. To her mind, her brother, Eddie, exhibited all the signs of an unrepentant reprobate.

Reprobate. Karen first heard that word when Reverend Andrews preached his sermon a few Sundays back. She looked it up in the big dictionary in the school library. It gave two meanings: (1) a rascal or scalawag in a humorous or affectionate sense; (2) someone predestined to damnation. Bingo! she'd thought. That second one fit Eddie to a T.

Sighing, she glanced down at her chipped plate and mismatched silverware, then looked hopefully at her mother.

"Ma, why don't you just serve it now? We're hungry. If it's cold when he gets here, he's got no one to blame but himself."

"What are you saying, child? We eat as a family unless there ain't no way around it."

Pa piped up. "That's right, Karen. You know the rules. Ain't that right, Mollie?"

Her mother's attention swiveled to him. "Never you mind, Earl. I don't need me no back-up." Her eyes shifted to his attire. "And why are you coming to the table wearing them long johns? That ain't fitting, and you know it."

Earl flinched and looked down. "Now, Mollie. You know I got to get up early, and I'll be heading to bed soon enough. I just thought this would save me a little time."

"I don't want to hear it, Earl. You go put something over them long johns right now."

Pa looked at Karen, but she just shrugged. Defeated, Pa rose from the table and went to change.

The noise of gravel crunching in the driveway and the revving of a 307 Chevy engine signaled Eddie's arrival. If that didn't provide enough clues, Karen thought, the radio blasting "Coal Miner's Daughter" clinched it.

The racket stopped, and the car door slammed. Through the window, Karen saw her sixteen-year-old brother bound up the steps, throw open the kitchen door, and saunter into the room. "Hey, Ma. Granny. Dinner ready?"

He looked over at Karen. "Hey, four-eyes."

Karen glared at him while Ma unleashed her head of steam. "Don't you 'Hi, Ma.' me. Dinner's been ready for the better part of an hour. Where the dickens have you been?"

Eddie ran a hand through his thick, blond hair and cast his blue eyes toward the floor. "I'm plumb sorry, Ma. It couldn't be helped. Old Man Compton high-centered his truck back apiece, and I just had to stop and help him get it out. I told him I needed to hurry home because a dinner made by the best danged cook in Garland County waited for me. That blamed hound of his growled at me, too. I don't know what its problem is. Anyway, I'm real sorry."

Eddie looked up at Ma and hit her with his best smile. That smile could melt Ma like butter on a hot griddle. "Well, helping out a neighbor in need is the Christian thing to do, like it say in the book of Luke. I reckon I can't be upset with you for being a Good Samaritan. Come here and give your mother a hug, then we'll eat. Karen, make sure Granny's got her teeth in."

Eddie looked over at Karen and tossed her a wink. While she scowled and ground her teeth, he hugged Ma and told her how nice she looked. Ma beamed and headed back in the kitchen. Karen shot daggers at Eddie, but she had to admit he really knew how to butter a biscuit.

Pa rejoined them, his long johns covered, and Ma returned with the pork chops, mashed potatoes, and mustard greens. During the meal, various conversations wove their way around the chewing and swallowing.

Pa talked baseball and how Detroit would be a sure winner in the AL pennant race. Eddie scoffed and said they didn't stand a chance against Oakland. Ma asked Eddie how the chops were. Eddie said they were the best he'd ever tasted. Granny's top denture fell out on her plate. Karen cleaned it off, got some Fixodent to spread on it, and helped her put it back in. Karen mentioned getting an A on her science project. Ma said, "That's nice. Don't forget to wash up the dishes before you go to bed." Eddie smirked. Ma said she wasn't much for politics, but she sure thought it good that a fine Republican like Nixon won out over that crybaby McGovern. Eddie agreed that Nixon definitely deserved it.

As the meal wound down, Pa looked at Eddie. "Son, I wonder if you'd mind helping me with the chores tomorrow evening. My lumbago done flared up on me something fierce."

"Gee, Pa, I wish I could, but football practice is in two-a-days now, and it's brutal. After that, I'm afraid I won't have nothing left."

Before Pa could speak, Ma jumped in. "That's right, Earl. You know how important Eddie is to the team. If they're gonna win the conference title this year, he's gotta take care of himself."

"Well, I think —"

Ma cut him off. "If you got to have some help with them chores, you can get Karen to do it."

Karen jumped up and slammed her palms on the table. "That is it! I've had all I can take. I'm sick to death of everyone catering to Eddie, treating him like some kind of royalty instead of what he is: a spoiled, lazy, obnoxious low-life."

In the stunned silence, she continued. "He doesn't do anything around here. He comes and goes when he wants, lies, makes lousy grades, skips class, and can't hold down even a part-time job. And what happens? You spend money you can ill afford to get him a car and gas money so he can drive around and act a hotshot."

She looked straight at her mother. "And all he has to do to keep getting away with it is sweet-talk you."

She turned to her father. "And Pa, you don't do anything about it because you're too buffaloed by Ma."

Her mother's mouth gaped like a catfish flopping on the bank, and her father's head hung down. Eddie's face seemed to be equal parts of alarm and anger.

Karen turned to her grandma. "Granny, I love you, and

I'm sorry you had to hear this, but it's been a long time coming."

Granny smiled at her and mumbled something. Karen leaned closer and heard, "Good on you, girl."

Karen hugged her, stood back up, and looked around the table. "I'm turning eighteen soon. I'll be able to get a full-time job and support myself. Maybe even go to the junior college if I can get a scholarship or student loan. And that's what I aim to do. Till then, I'm getting my clothes and going to stay with my friend Ellen and her family. They were nice enough to accept me when I asked. I knew this day was coming. I just didn't know when."

Karen fought back the tears she knew would flow later. "Ma. Pa. I love you, and I'm thankful for my raising, but I can't go on like this." Her voice cracked. "I won't. I hope some things change around here, but that's not up to me."

Karen went to her room and took her suitcase from her closet. As she left the house and started down the lane to the road, she met Jeb Compton driving up in his truck.

Jeb pulled the truck to a halt and rolled down the window. "Hello, Miss Karen. Looks like you be heading somewhere."

"Hello, Mr. Compton. Yes, I'm going to the Randolphs' house."

Jeb mulled that over, noting the suitcase Karen clenched in her hands. "Far piece to be walking. No one to give you a ride?"

Karen teared up. "No, sir. I didn't ask."

"Well, stow your case behind the seat and hop in front. Just shove Homer over some. As soon as I have a few words with your folks, I'll take you there."

Karen wasn't sure if Mr. Compton could make anything better. If she was being honest, she hoped her family would wrap her up in their arms and welcome her back.

"I said a few things my folks didn't want to hear when I left, Mr. Compton," she said.

"Well," Jeb said, "we all say things."

Karen climbed in the cab of the truck, and Homer plopped his big head on her knee. She closed her eyes, letting the sound of the engine calm her nerves.

When they pulled up to the house, Karen looked it over. She knew ever stick of wood that made it, every drop of paint. But now, it looked like someone's else's house, a place like a dozen others in this town.

Jeb killed the engine, hopped out to open Karen's door. She took a few seconds getting out. It seemed like to her, whatever happened next, could change her whole life. She wasn't sure if she was ready.

# CHAPTER 16 — CALL TO ORDER

The sunrise found Jeb Compton sitting in his white oak rocker on his porch. He usually wasn't there to greet the sun, but last night, dreams of his dearly departed Annie unsettled his sleep and caused him to rise earlier than usual. Jeb flipped the pages of the *Hurlin Express* and took an occasional pull from his morning bottle of Coors. He'd be danged if he'd let a high-priced doctor tell him not to have his beer, and anyway it was a mighty rare day when he had more than one.

Jeb looked over at Homer who was launching an all-out assault on a nervy gopher in the nearby garden. Red clay soil, rocks, and a few onions flew as the bluetick hound's large paws followed the route laid out for him.

"Hey, Homer, give it a rest, will you? You're tearing up more things than the gopher."

Homer gave an indignant snort, but he stopped and came

over to the porch. Jeb brushed the dirt off his hound's muzzle. "There, you look a mite more respectable now. Say, I see where the paper has a article on the lifelong doings of Judge Burnside. You've not met him, but he be a good man. He spent many years judging in that there courtroom, and he were as honest and fair as a man can be. Now that he's retired, I wonder what he's doing with his time."

The Honorable Judge Morton T. Burnside, dressed in a tweed suit and sporting a tie with blue pinstripes, walked into The Roundup. He doffed his hat, handed it to the bartender, nodded to the customers, and headed for the back room. Establishing himself behind the podium, he peered around the assembled men through Coke-bottle lenses. As far as his poor old eyes could tell, it looked like all the usual suspects were present. They were scattered around his podium in fold-up chairs and were already arguing. Judge Burnside shook his head. He'd better get this party started, he thought and slammed his gavel against the sounding block three times. The room grew quiet.

"I hereby call this meeting of the Hurlin Debating Society to order. Clem, would you please read the minutes of the last meeting?"

A short, pot-bellied man with glasses rose from his chair. "I'd be happy to, Judge."

Clem James, the town barber, pulled a fat wad of folded paper from his back pocket. The irony of Clem being bald as an egg and responsible for most of the men's hair in Hurlin did not escape him, and he ran a hand over his pink scalp. He unfolded the packet, shuffled through the pages till he found the one he sought, cleared his throat, and commenced reading.

"It say here that last week we was debating what to do about them socialists what are creeping into Congress. Caleb suggested we recruit Hank Williams, Jr. and put him up in the next election. He can sing, plus, he won't go messing with our freedoms."

Clem took his seat, pulled a pencil from his pocket, and prepared to take notes for tonight's meeting.

"Thank you, Clem," the judge said. He cleared his throat. "Now then, for tonight's discussion, I offer up the curious case of James Barnswallow. As you know, if you've been following the local news, James was found dead in his living room, his body reduced to ash, with nothing left but his hands and feet. The police say the only part of his house that burned was a small patch on the wood floor beneath him. The state fire marshal thinks it might be a case of spontaneous combustion. Now, for an object to combust, two things are required: a heat source and a flammable substance. I open the floor. What does this illustrious group have to say about that?"

Luke Maness, tall, spare, and the proprietor of the local Ace Hardware store, stood up. The Judge released the breath he hadn't realized he'd been holding. Thank goodness Luke was speaking, he thought. Luke was a bit of a know-it-all, but he had a level head. He could set the tone for the session, and reason might reign.

"Heck, Judge, we all know Bob was a heavy drinker and smoker. I'll bet he got drunk on Jim Beam and passed out on the floor. The alcohol likely spilled on him, and his lit cigarette set him on fire."

Luke, grinning, took his chair. The Judge had seen that same grin many times on the local prosecuting attorney when he thought he had an open-and-shut case.

"Eminently logical, Luke, but does it explain why the fire didn't spread to the rest of the house or why just his hands and feet were left?"

Luke's grin faded a bit.

Just then, Caleb Brown, short, bearded, and wearing a mustard-stained shirt that strained at the belly, stood up. The Judge's own stomach gave a little twist, and he tried not to wince. Would the affable owner of Caleb's Bait & More be on his game tonight, he wondered, or had he been knocking back one too many Coors?

"Good point, your honor. I've got me another idea," Caleb said. "Jim had a problem with gas something fierce. Shoot, his farts could clear a room." There were murmurs of agreement in the crowd, and he continued. "I'll bet he built up a good supply in his guts and some of them, um, them things that speed up the break-down of stuff —"

"I believe the word you're looking for is bacteria."

"Thank you, Judge. Yeah, I'll bet them bacteria built up enough heat to set off a spark. That lit up the gas, and it burned through Jim from the inside out. Lots of fat in his body for fuel." Caleb took his seat and looked around for support of his theory.

"Not bad, Caleb," the Judge said. "You may have hit on something there. It's happened with bales of hay. Well, not the gas part."

Caleb beamed at the judge, and Joe Whitson stood up. The judge's stomach tightened. Joe, all sharp angles and bony features, had a reputation as an ardent conspiracy theory buff, as had the victim. Since Joe's wife had left him and taken up with the first man who paid her some attention, he'd only gotten worse.

"I reckon the government was responsible. Old Jim never

quit raising a stink about government plots in his Letters to the Editor down at the *Hurlin Express*. I'll bet he hit too close to home with one of them, and they sent out one of them Black Ops teams to shut him up permanent like."

Luke shot to his feet. "That's ridiculous. We need to be serious here."

Joe barked back. "It is not ridiculous. Luke don't know how far them government goons will go to cover stuff up."

Judge Burnside winced as his stomach gave a sharp twinge. Why me, Lord? he thought as he slammed down his gavel. "I will have order here, gentlemen. Now, Luke, Joe has the floor. If you want to argue with his point, it will have to wait."

"Joe, do you have anything to add?"

"No, sir. I'm done."

"That's interesting, Joe, but I think we should concentrate more on the how than the why. Why don't you mull that over for a while and see what you come up with? Does anyone else have anything else to offer?"

Bart Scoggins, the elementary peewee football coach, jumped to his feet. His muscular torso and neat crewcut contrasted the confused look in his eyes. The confusion likely had something to do with the hits he took to the head when he played semi-pro ball. The blows left him a little light in the lunch box, but it didn't matter since he put together a winning team every year.

The judge's stomach gurgled, loud enough to be heard, just as Coach Bart started to speak.

"Well, Judge, I think those guys are way off base. I keep telling y'all that we're not alone. There are aliens among us. They are always studying us with them anal probes and such. I'll bet they experimented on old Jim and zapped him with a laser when they was done just to cover up their tracks.

They're sneaky like that."

Bart plopped back down in his chair and sat there mumbling to himself.

The Judge's stomach rumbled again, louder this time. He thought he heard muffled laughter coming from the front row but decided to ignore it.

"Gentlemen, we've had a stimulating discussion, but I'm afraid I have another engagement. I call for an adjournment and suggest we keep up with the news to see if there are further developments. Goodnight, and thank you for coming."

The judge rushed past a few of the men whose hands were outstretched, tapping his watch to indicate he was late for his next commitment. Coach Bart slapped him on the back, a move that nearly caused the judge to have an unseemly accident. He watched as several of the men headed for the bar, and envied them their good stomachs. He walked carefully out the door, heading for home and the medicine cabinet, thinking about James Barnswallow's inelegant demise, and hoping none of the theories he heard tonight were right.

## CHAPTER 17 — FAMILY JEWELS

Homer shot through the gap between Jeb Compton's legs, evading Jeb's attempted grab at his collar. By the time Jeb got his balance and turned around, the big bluetick hound sat facing him on the ground ten feet away, his tongue lolling. "Dadgummit, Homer, I know you're not hopped up to go the vet, but it's time for your rabies shot."

Homer huffed.

"Now, it be for your own protection," Jeb continued. "With all them critters you skedaddle after, you been bit a time or two, and you don't never know what all they carry."

Homer appeared unswayed by Jeb's logic.

"All right then. I'm tired of chasing you. I'll have to go with plan B."

That plan consisted of Jeb going to the kitchen and returning with a plate of leftover biscuits and a small jar of sorghum molasses. Jeb sat down on the porch and set the items on the small oak table by his chair. He looked over at Homer. "You hungry, boy?"

Homer sat rooted, his eyes glued to the plate. The hound had a prodigious appetite, but his fear of capture warred with his craving for biscuits. Jeb picked up a copy of the *Hurlin Express* from the floor and commenced reading. Homer edged closer but remained off the porch. Jeb set the newspaper in his lap, reached over, and picked up a biscuit. He poured some molasses on it and took a bite. "Not too bad, if I do say so. Sure you don't want some?"

Homer licked his muzzle, whined, and gave up the fight. He hopped up on the porch and slowly came toward Jeb. Jeb tossed the rest of the biscuit on the floor, and Homer pounced, consuming it in one gulp. Jeb smiled. "Good, huh? Here, have you another."

He held out a biscuit, and as Homer came to take it, Jeb snagged his collar. "Sorry to trick you, Homer, but you left me no choice. Here, eat this one, and then we be on our way."

Homer's eyes seemed mournful, but his mouth accepted the biscuit. In short order, they arrived at the Westside Animal Clinic. Jeb wrestled Homer's leash on, and with no small effort, got Homer through the clinic door. Blessed be, Jeb thought as he scanned the room and saw no other animals in attendance.

The receptionist, a plump, middle-aged woman with frizzy, permed hair and large hoop earrings, looked up. "Oh Lord, is it already time for that one again?"

Homer had a well-deserved reputation at the clinic, in large part due to the unfortunate incident with their office cat. "Yes, ma'am," Jeb said. "I'm afraid it be so."

The woman sniffed. "Well, take a seat over there. Doctor Prentice will be with you shortly."

Jeb thanked her and led Homer to the row of chairs by the window. He sat down and eyed the stack of magazines on the battered wooden table. He spied a copy of the *Farm Journal.* The cover story, "Give Soybeans the Upper Hand," caught his attention, and he started to reach for the magazine. With his hand halfway there, he stopped. I'd best not, he thought. When Homer's at the vet, he needs my undivided attention. Maybe, if things go passable, they be willing to let me borrow it.

In a few minutes, the receptionist caught Jeb's attention. "Go to the middle examining room, please."

Jeb stood up, braced himself, and half-walked, half-dragged a protesting Homer to their destination. He took a seat on one of the plastic chairs in front of the stainless-steel table. He surveyed the glass-fronted cabinets lining the wall that held an assortment of drugs and equipment. The rear door to the room opened, and a short, spare young man with dishwater-blond hair entered. Jeb noticed that, behind his glasses, his gray eyes looked weary, and the white lab coat looked a bit rumpled.

The doctor smiled. "Mr. Compton, how are you?"

"Fair to middlin', Doc, but you be looking a trifle worn around the edges."

Dr. Prentice grimaced. "I spent a good part of the night with one of Lem Dawson's cows. She tried to give birth on her own, but it was a breech, and she had a hard time of it."

"I hope she be okay."

"I'm happy to report that cow and calf are both doing fine." The vet turned his attention to Homer. "Now then, Homer, how are you today?"

Homer did his level best to burrow between Jeb's legs and hide under the chair. "He be fine in general, Doc. Just needs a check-me-up and his s.h.o.t.s."

Jeb spelled out the word 'shots' like a mother might do with her small child. Nonetheless, Homer gave a pitiful whine.

Jeb lifted a protesting Homer onto the exam table, and Dr. Prentice came around the tail-end of it with a thermometer in hand. "If you'll get a good grip on him, we'll start by getting one unpleasantry out of the way."

Jeb gripped Homer's head and winced in sympathy as the tail got lifted and the thermometer inserted. After several seconds, the vet said, "Perfectly normal, Homer. Now, let me check your impressive ears." About fifteen minutes later, the vet finished up. "We'll check his blood work and mail you the results, but everything looks good. There is one matter we need to discuss, though."

"What's that, Doc?"

"Have you given any thought to having Homer fixed?"

Jeb looked puzzled. "Fixed, Doc? Fixed how?" Dr. Prentice used his forefinger and middle finger to make a snipping motion. Realization hit as an equal mix of shock and concern showed on Jeb's face, and at the same time, Homer let out a low growl.

Oblivious, the vet continued. "We'd anesthetize him, of course. It won't take much time, and healing is fairly rapid."

Jeb held up his hand in a warning motion. "Ease up a minute, Doc. What brung this on?"

"Well, unwanted animals are a problem, and there are a lot of strays. People are always dumping animals. Our town's shelter is full of them. They don't like to euthanize the animals, but it's expensive to board them, and the amount of space available is limited. We're trying to help with the problem by getting as many pets spayed and neutered as possible."

"But I don't be planning on getting rid of Homer, so

there's no real need for him getting fixed."

"Well, you're forgetting one thing."

"What's that?"

Dr. Prentice took off his glasses with one hand and rubbed his eyes with the other. "Your hound might have a good home, Mr. Compton, but his breed is known to roam far and wide. If he happens to find a female friend on his travels, isn't it possible there would soon be some little Homers running around? And, if there were, would someone want to keep them or would they be gotten rid of one way or the other?"

Jeb ran a hand through his hair. "I never give the matter no thought, Doc, but I be seeing the truth in what you're saying." Homer whined as if he was following the conversation. "Tell you what. Can I take me some time to think it over?"

"Of course, Mr. Compton. It's not like I can force you to do it. If you decide to go ahead, we can schedule Homer's appointment."

Driving home, Jeb rolled down the window partway so the hound could stick his head out. Homer, however, did not avail himself of the opportunity.

Jeb looked over. "Something the matter, old boy? Don't be worrying about what Doc say. It ain't like you got a lady friend somewhere." Homer hung his head and whined. Jeb's eyebrows raised. "Homer, look at me. You don't, now do you?" Homer wouldn't meet Jeb's eyes. "Well, I be swan. I had no idea it were like that. Ain't nothing to be ashamed of, but after what the vet said, it do put a whole new slant on the matter."

When they arrived home, Homer took off, and Jeb went to the kitchen to make a phone call. After hanging up, he stood on the porch and called for Homer. The hound came

117

bounding through the field and up on the porch. "Homer, let me tell you straight up: I've decided that the right thing to do is getting you fixed."

Whether the tone of his voice or Homer's understanding of English came through, the hound threw back his head and let out an anguished bawl.

"Now don't be taking it so hard. Here's what we're gonna do." The hound stopped his bawl and stared at Jeb. "I just got off the phone with that breeder fella what my sweet Annie got you from. He say he's got a female bluetick who's ready to mate, and he be looking for a suitable male. Do you know somebody to fit that bill?"

Jeb had Homer's undivided attention. "Thought you might be interested. I'll take you over there tomorrow and leave you with him for a few days. It should make parting with your — well, it might make things a bit easier for you, and you'd be passing on your line."

Homer chuffed, a sign Jeb took as his assent, bounded off the porch, and headed for the field.

That night, Jeb fell into a reverie, reliving the last Christmas he shared with Annie. She was already sick by then with the cancer that finally took her. And yet, somehow, she'd conspired to hunt down a pup to surprise him with. How much effort had that taken, Jeb wondered?

Jeb pulled out the photo album he kept on the shelf above his stash of bath towels. Inside, he found the photos he wanted — three pages from that Christmas. There was Annie with a headscarf around her head, her eyes bright with happiness, and there was Homer with his big ears and clumsy paws.

"This was the best present I ever got in my whole danged life, Annie," Jeb said.

The tears that fell next would have ruined those priceless

pictures, had Annie not had the foresight to house them behind a sheet of plastic.

## CHAPTER 18 — TEN CATS

A white car with the Arkansas Health Department logo on the door bumped down Jeb Compton's lane. As it reached the end, the driver spotted a tall man with a big dog on the porch of the house and stopped the car.

Homer, the big bluetick hound, bounded off the porch and homed in on the vehicle, bawling his hunting cry. Jeb, who'd drifted off, woke from his nap with a start and looked around, seeing Homer approach the unfamiliar car. By the time Jeb reached him, Homer had his front paws on the driver's window, peering intently inside the car.

Jeb grabbed Homer's collar and yanked the dog back. Seeing the large animal controlled, the driver hesitantly rolled down his window. "Excuse me, sir, but I came here looking for directions when that feral dog attacked. I asked a man who tended a herd of goats; he didn't know the location

I'm seeking, but he said you might be able to help."

Jeb smiled. "Well, first off, let me say sorry for this here ornery hound. He just can't seem to help himself, but he ain't feral. Just protecting what's his. Second, who might you be looking for?"

The man consulted his clipboard full of papers. "Uh, this gives Betsy Deveraux at 115 Mockingbird Lane. Do you know her?"

Jeb nodded. "I know of her. She's the one with all them cats. I had planned to go say howdy when she moved here, but when I seen her cats, I turned right around and skedaddled. You see, I had Homer along with. Him and cats get along about as good as a fox and a hen. Anyway, I do recollect how to get over there."

After following the directions, the government man finally pulled to a stop in Betsy Deveraux's driveway. He pinned his name tag — proclaiming Stanley Heath in capital letters — on his jacket, straightened his tie and adjusted his glasses, grabbed his clipboard and pen, and put on his "official" face. He marched up the three oak steps to the porch, rapped on the door, and stiffly waited for someone to emerge.

Someone did, and he started at the sight. Betsy Deveraux, slightly bent over, presented herself. She wore a ratty old robe with various stains on it, house slippers that may have been pink at some point, and stringy gray hair in desperate need of a wash dangling down over her grimy face. She wore a crumpled cap that looked to have been sat on, and she held a gnarly wooden cane. Worst of all, though, was her smell, a mixture of ammonia and sweat, and Stanley struggled not to gag.

"Howdy, sonny," Betsy said. "How are you this fine day?"

Stanley attempted to answer, but the stench caused him to take a step backward. He fumbled for his handkerchief, used it to wipe his watering eyes, then held it over his nose. "I'm Stanley Heath from the Department of Health," he said from beneath the white cloth.

"Yes, I can see that from your fancy badge, there. What can I do for you, Stanley?"

"There have been some complaints filed with our office, and I've been sent to check out the situation."

"What kind of complaints?" Betsy asked. "Far as I know, I ain't bothered nobody."

"Why don't we start with some questions, ma'am?" He held up his clipboard for her to see, but the pen slid from it and clattered to the porch. He felt his ears turn red, and he bent down to retrieve it, but it had disappeared between a gap in the oak floor boards.

"That's okay," she said. "I've got a pen you can use. Don't get too many people around here, much less important folk like you. Why don't you come in and set a spell?"

Stanley could only imagine the horrors that waited if he crossed the threshold. He stood there a moment, frozen with indecision, then shook himself and said, "Uh, maybe we could do this on the porch."

She smiled. "But don't you have to do an inspection?"

Stanley flinched. "Well, normally I would," he said and paused. "But, uh, it's so nice out here, I think we can take care of it in the fresh air."

"Suit yourself, but I was going to bring you some sweet tea and homemade cookies. It's only neighborly."

Horrified at the thought of what those cookies contained, Stanley thought furiously. He could feel the gears of his brain grind together. Think! he told himself. Suddenly inspiration hit. "I'd love to, but I'm a diabetic, you see. Can't have sweets. The sugar and all." He looked at her hopefully.

"Well, okay then, but you don't mind if I fetch some for

me, do you? I could use me a little pick-me-up."

"No, no, that would be fine."

"Okay then, I'll just go fix me some. Won't take long. Sure you don't want to come inside."

"Oh, no," he said. "Out here is splendid."

Stanley sat waiting in the white oak chair, breathing deeply of the fresh air and trying to unclog his lungs from the residual miasma he'd taken in. They don't pay me enough to put up with this, he thought, but I've still to get enough information to fill out the forms.

Soon, the door opened. Stanley braced for the interaction and kept the handkerchief close, just in case. As she emerged on the porch, his mouth fell open.

In front of him stood an attractive woman of middle age. She had short blonde hair, cut in pageboy fashion, a pretty blue dress with a flowery print, and black loafers. She flashed him a grin as she came over and took the chair beside him. "It is nice out here."

Stanley stammered. "But, but, where is Betsy Deveraux?"

"Oh, her? She went away for a while, and I'm taking her place."

Stanley continued to stare. "You?" he said.

"I'm sorry I tricked you, but I get such a kick out of the reactions I see."

"But how?" He inadvertently took a breath, and noticed that the ammonia smell was nearly gone.

The grin returned. "I keep an old robe saturated with ammonia. Most folks don't notice the subtle difference between it and cat urine. I stained it up with whatnot and never wash it. The grizzly gray hair is a wig, of course, and the hat and slippers I found at the Goodwill shop in town. Then, a few strokes of brown shoe polish on my face and some nose plugs complete the look. I keep all the fixings in a box in the garage, and I can change in and out of costume in no time. Impressed?"

Stanley sat there in stunned silence for a minute as he tried to process. "But why?"

"I'm kind of a loner, and I like my privacy. As a writer, I sort of require that. I found that putting on that persona and puttering around outside with a few of my kitties works wonders. The neighbors are good enough to help me out by passing it on. Stanley, never underestimate the power of gossip in a small town."

"So, you don't have —" He consulted his clipboard, flipping through the pages till he found what he wanted, "ten cats?"

"Oh, I do. At the moment. It varies over time, as some pass on and new ones mysteriously appear on my porch."

"Don't you find that a little peculiar?"

"Nope. It started with Lady Florence. She's a grey Maltese, and I found her on a walk one day. She was expecting, and clearly abandoned, so I took her home where she soon gave birth to four adorable kittens. After she finished with her nursing, I took her to the vet and had her spayed, as I did with each kitten when it came of age. Anyway, that put me to five right off the bat. The others, as I mentioned, came over time. I took them all in, provided them food and companionship, and loved them. They gave me the family I never really had. All of them are current on their shots and will stay that way. Any other questions?"

Stanley thought a moment. "But the smell —"

"You're free to come inside and check for yourself. Yes, they produce copious amounts of odor, but I keep that confined to one bathroom where their litter boxes reside. I clean them every day and use fresh litter frequently, so the smell is minimized. Most of the time, it's not bad at all."

Stanley shook his head. "It must cost you a small fortune."

"It's worth it to me. I did mention I am a writer?" Stanley nodded. "Turns out I'm a pretty successful one."

"I see. Well, that does it for me." He smiled, and it softened the stern look he'd so carefully crafted. "I'm going to fill out the forms, and ask you to sign them. As far as I'm concerned, that will be that."

She smiled. "Thank you for that. I know I said I'm a loner, but I do appreciate a good conversation from time to time. Why don't you come in and stay awhile. Get to meet my little family, and maybe indulge in the tea and cookies I offered. If, as I suspect, the diabetic thing was something you made up on the spur of the moment."

Stanley laughed. "I think I'll take you up on that. Let me just finish up and get you to sign these papers." When she finished, Stanley glanced at her signature. His eyebrows shot up. "You're her?" he asked.

She smiled and winked. "Full of surprises, aren't I?"

"But you are famous! You are one of my favorite authors. You –"

Realizing how he must sound to her, Stanley flushed and clamped his teeth together to stop gushing. She just smiled.

"Aww, thanks. I'm glad you like my books."

Stanley blew out a breath. "I'll say. But, how on earth did best-selling author, Betsy Chapple, end up in a small town like Hurlin? You've been on *The New York Times* top ten list with three of your last four novels."

Betsy frowned. "You noticed that, did you? I'm still kind of miffed about *Cerulean Sky* not making it, and I'm trying to figure out where I could have improved it."

"Well, I thought it was great," Stanley said.

Betsy smiled. "You're kind. As for how I ended up in Hurlin –

She paused and thought about the question. "I was born and raised here. My high school English teacher saw something in me and got me started writing. I left Hurlin when I moved to New York to hone my craft. That big city can chew you up and spit you out. When things got rough, and I needed a place to heal, I found myself coming home. Now I use it to get away from the grind and work on my next book. You may not know it, Stanley, but this town is a comfort to me. Like my cats."

Stanley's eyes clouded over. "Well, thank you for sharing that. It means a lot to me."

Betsy smiled. "I like you, Stanley. Now, how about those cookies?"

# Chapter 19 — Empathy

Jeb Compton hollered from his front porch. "Homer! Hey, where you at, boy?"

The large head of his bluetick hound emerged from the field grass where he'd been nosing after a covey of quail.

"I got to run over to the clinic and see Doc Wilkens about this blamed poison ivy rash. It just keeps spreading, and it's itching me something fierce. Try to stay out of trouble till I get back." Homer barked once, ducked back in the grass and resumed his activity.

As Jeb drove and scratched, he thought about his first visit. He'd brought his Annie to the clinic after she'd been feeling poorly for a while and didn't perk up like she usually did. They didn't know she had cancer, but Doc picked up on that real quick after a round of tests. He'd been a little too cold and clinical for Jeb's taste, but Annie liked him for not sugar-coating it or making false promises. That made Doc golden in Jeb's book.

The dented '62 Chevy rattled into the parking lot of the Hurlin clinic, the radio blaring Charley Pride's new single, "Kiss An Angel Good Morning." The worn tires crunched on the gravel as the truck came to a halt. Zeke Farrell, a beefy man, short in stature, cautiously eased himself from the seat of his truck and hobbled over to the three-step wooden stairs. He grabbed the railing, slowly pulled himself up to the door, and entered. Sadie Jones, the nurse/receptionist at the small four-room clinic, sat at her desk arranging her collection of troll dolls. She jumped up and helped Zeke to the back room, where she took his weight and blood pressure. Then she escorted him into the examining room. Doc Wilkens looked up and grimaced.

"What's the problem, Zeke?"

Zeke let out a groan. "It's my lumbago, Doc. I tell ya, I ain't able to take much more of this. With all them ruts in the road, the drive over here near about finished me."

Doc sighed. "Don't exaggerate, Zeke. You've been here with this plenty of times, and you've always managed to survive. What triggered it this time?"

Zeke frowned. "Lucy. She had me tote a bag of chicken feed from the barn to the roost. Dad-blamed woman knows I got a bad back, and she made me do it anyway."

If Zeke came looking for sympathy, he'd come to the wrong place. "Come on, Zeke. Those bags of feed weigh fifty pounds at least. Surely, you don't expect that slip of a woman to lug it by herself." Zeke muttered something to himself but said nothing the doctor could hear. "All right, then," Doc Wilkens said. "Take off your shirt and lie face down on the examining table."

After much groaning, Zeke worked his way onto the table. Doc commenced pushing and prodding Zeke's lower back, prompting a yowl of protest.

"Geeze-oh-Pete, Doc! You trying to cripple me your own self? Bread dough ain't been kneaded that much."

"Stop your complaining. I'm only doing what's necessary to determine if there is any noticeable change from the last time you were here." He gave Zeke's back a final poke. "And there's not. I'll give you an epidural for the pain."

"Sadie," he called out, please prepare a syringe with forty milliliters of Methylprednisolone."

Sadie popped her head in the door. "That's the Dep-Medrol, right?"

"That's correct."

Sadie returned with Zeke's chart and the syringe and handed them to Doc, who had Zeke lying on the table curled into a "C" shape to give the doctor the best view of his spine.

"Sadie, please remain," Doc said. "I have to place the injection very carefully, and I need you to help keep Zeke from moving." Sadie nodded and got a good grip on the patient. Doc administered the shot. "Okay, Zeke, you can put your shirt on. Keep taking that anti-inflammatory I prescribed, and have Lucy continue giving you those heat treatments."

Zeke frowned. "Shoot, Doc, you know none of them things do me much good for long. Ain't you got something else I can try?"

Doc trained piercing blue eyes on Zeke. "If you recall, I suggested you lose at least thirty pounds to take some strain off your back."

He flipped through Zeke's chart. "According to this, you've gained three pounds."

Zeke looked down. "I tried to lose some, Doc, but it just ain't working."

Doc sighed. "Then I've done all I can for you. The only thing left is to see a specialist in Little Rock. I can give you the name of a good one if you want to go that route."

"Ain't no way I can do that, Doc. It'll cost too blamed much."

"In that case, Zeke, you better get busy losing some weight."

After Zeke left, Nurse Sadie's permed brown hair bounced as she shook her head. She pinned Doc with a stare. "You're a good doctor, but I swear, you have got to work on your attitude. You've got the bedside manner of a cornered possum."

Doc's voice took a warning tone. "Sadie," he started and then thought better of continuing. Though annoyed, he bit his tongue. He'd already had two nurses quit on him. "You could be right, but I can't generate much patience for people who whine and complain but won't do anything to help themselves."

Sadie tried again. "Still, he was hurting. You could have been a mite easier on him." Doc gave a noncommittal grunt and changed the subject. "Is there anyone in the waiting room?"

"No, not right now."

"Then I'm going out back for a smoke break." Avoiding Sadie's disapproving look, he went out the front door and down the steps. He walked the dirt path to the back, thumped down on the rusted metal chair, pulled a pack of Marlboros from his shirt pocket, and lit up. He sucked in a lungful of cigarette smoke then blew out a plume.

Damn, he thought, not only is Sadie on my bad side, I'm starting to run off patients, and I guess I could have been nicer to Zeke. He took another drag on his cigarette and noticed a gray squirrel scratching in the dirt for a stashed acorn. When the squirrel found his prize, he clutched it in his tiny paws, sat up, and stared at Doc. Doc spoke to the squirrel. "Sadie means well, but she doesn't understand how it is."

"So, how is it?"

Doc jerked his head toward the voice. Sadie was standing there. "Sadie! You could give a man a heart attack! What are you doing back here?"

Sadie smiled, but it didn't reach her eyes. "You left before we could finish our discussion, so I thought I'd come back here so we could take care of that. Now, what is it I don't understand?"

Doc tried deflection. He looked toward the back door of the clinic. "What if we have more patients show up?"

"We're through with our appointments for the day, and we can hear the gravel crunching if any other patients stop by. Now, back to my question."

"I thought I made it pretty clear I didn't want to talk about it."

"Yes, and I think it's pretty clear that we need to talk about it. Just try. Please."

The "please" got to him. Doc sighed. What the hell, he thought as he stood up. "Okay, but you take the chair. I need to pace." After Sadie sat down, he framed his thoughts, then started in. "I finished my BS by twenty-two, my MD by twenty-six, my internship by twenty-seven, and my residency by twenty-nine. I was ready to move mountains, but the draft and Vietnam had other ideas. My 'attitude,' as you call it, formed during my tour of duty at the 2nd MASH unit at An

Khe in sixty-six. There were sixty beds when I was there, and we had more than a thousand surgical cases in less than a year. Pain, complications, and worse occurred with alarming regularity. I had to harden myself. If I hadn't, if I'd let all the pain and suffering of those men affect me, I'd have gone over the edge. And I wouldn't have been the first."

Sally looked at him. "I can't imagine how bad that must have been."

Doc quit pacing and stared at the ground. "I still have nightmares. I thought things would get better back in the States, but instead, they just turned in a different direction. I took a position at a Fort Smith hospital. The patient load was tremendous; they came in a steady stream. The hospital emphasized efficiency, with the concentration on diagnosis, prognosis, and treatment. Biopsies, blood tests, scans, calls from emergency room doctors — never time to turn around."

He rubbed the back of his neck as he resumed pacing.

"In the midst of all that, you had to find a few minutes for each patient. A few minutes! No time for understanding and responding to their feelings. No time for empathy, listening, and communication. The next patient needed to be seen."

He spun around and stared at Sadie. Apparently alarmed, the squirrel that appeared to have been listening to their exchange scampered off. "And do you want to know the irony of it? My "attitude" that maintained my sanity in Vietnam, and following the hospital's own directives, cost me that job. Patient complaints of lack of caring, compassion, and empathy did me in."

Sadie crossed her arms. "So you came here."

He blew out a breath. "Yes. I thought things might be different in a smaller town. Less, I don't know, hectic, maybe."

"And?"

"And it's still the same. I've got time now to get to know my patients. To talk to them, understand their concerns and fears, and show some compassion, but —"

"But?"

"Luke 4:23 says, 'Physician, heal thyself.' But I can't seem to shake off what I've become."

"Do you want to?"

Doc's eyes widened. "Lord, yes!"

Sadie smiled, and this time, it reached her eyes. "Then we'll work on it. You don't have to do this alone. That's why you have a nurse."

Doc grimaced. "That might be above your pay grade."

"Well, then, you'll just have to give me a raise." The crunching of gravel stopped their conversation. Sadie walked to the edge of the building and peeped around. "Looks like Jeb Compton's old truck." She turned back to Doc. "Ready for our next patient?"

Doc sucked in a deep breath. He thought about Jeb and that dog he always talked about. He thought about Jeb's late wife, Annie, and how hard it had been to tell them she had cancer. He squared his shoulders. "I think I might just be," he said.

## Chapter 20 — Responsibility

Jeb stepped onto his porch and called for his hound. Homer came tearing around the corner of the house and skidded to a halt, almost over-balancing. Jeb shook his head and grinned. "Do I even want to know what you done been up to?" Homer looked the soul of innocence. "Well, anyway, I just got a call from the breeder. He said that his female bluetick — you know the one — just gave birth to a litter of four pups.

"Since you had a hand in that, what say we go over there and take a look at your offspring? I'll bet them pups is a sight to behold." Homer seemed all for the idea, so they loaded up in Jeb's truck cab and took off down the lane.

Jeb glanced over at Homer and rested his hand on the big hound's head. "You know, Homer, Annie and me could never have no kids, and we both wished it otherwise. I'm glad you had the chance we never did."

Zeke Farrell pushed his chair back from the table, groaned, and rubbed his ample belly. "Them was good eats, Lucy, but I might a overdid it a tad; I'm full as a tick. I'm going to be needing to let my belt out a few notches."

Lucy gave an unladylike snort. "I can't imagine why. You packed away two full helpings and were eyeing a third. As for your belt, it looks like it's on the last notch now. 'Sides, didn't Doc tell you to lose some weight to help with your bad back?"

Zeke scowled. "I can't lose weight when you put them kind a eats on the table. As for that old stony-faced grump, he don't know half what he thinks he do."

Lucy drew herself up to her full five-foot height and pinned Zeke with a glare. Sparks appeared to form in her eyes — the kind seen when sharpening a lawnmower blade on a grinder. "Which would still leave him knowing twice as much as you. So, this is my fault for my cooking or Doc's fault for you not listening to him? I've had it with you always having to blame other folks for your own problems."

Zeke held up both hands. "Now, Lucy."

"Don't 'Now Lucy' me! It's way past time for you to take responsibility for your own actions."

The 1952 Hurlin Tigers capped off an undefeated season with a 28-17 thumping of the Mt. Ida Lions, and senior fullback Zeke Farrell had scored the touchdown that put the game on ice with under two minutes to play. As the team left the locker room, Zeke spotted his girlfriend Lucy Milton with some of the other members of the marching band. She knelt by the sidelines, putting her flute away in its case.

Zeke ran over. "Hey, you. Did you see my last touchdown?"

Lucy, a small girl with delicate features and shiny black hair, looked up. "Hey. Yeah, that was something all right!"

Zeke, not tall but built like a fireplug, smiled. "It sure were. Coach Benson called it the play of the game. I ain't sure about that. There was my other touchdown, and I'd a scored a third if them dang blockers had done their jobs."

"So, I guess you're going to go celebrate with the team?"

"Better believe it! Sam managed to round up a couple of kegs, and we be heading down to the river bottoms. You're coming, ain't ya?"

"I can't, but Zeke —"

"Yeah?"

"Can we go sit in the bleachers for a few minutes before you leave?"

Zeke looked puzzled, but he agreed. On their way over, he exchanged some hoorahs with a few fans. Lucy sat down on the first row at the far end of the empty bleachers, but he felt too excited to sit. "Okay, what's up?"

Lucy looked at her lap for so long it seemed she would never speak.

"Hey, Lucy, come on," Zeke said. "You can talk to me. Are you feeling low?" he asked, although he felt as if his performance in the game should have had her sitting on Cloud Nine.

Lucy looked across the bleachers. The stands were as empty as an abandoned silo. "Zeke," she said," I'm going to have a baby."

Zeke's powerful legs that had propelled him to so many touchdowns suddenly struggled to keep him upright. "No," he said, "that can't be right. It was only that one time! Say, are you sure?"

Lucy's temper flared. "Of course, I'm sure. I've been throwing up in the morning for two weeks straight. Plus, there's other ways of knowing."

"Like what?"

Lucy's cheeks turned red, and she looked off toward the visitor's goal post. "I haven't had my monthly visitor in a while."

Zeke's heart had dropped to his stomach. "Could it be some kind a bug."

Lucy sighed, and when she spoke, she sounded like she was talking to a little kid. "Zeke, I know what this is. A girl just knows."

Zeke stood with his arms akimbo. "Okay, then." His heart was a drum. "And you're sure it's mine?"

Lucy gasped. "You crumb! You spent nearly a year talking me into this. Zeke, you said you loved me! And now you ask if I did it with somebody else."

Zeke felt as if a cage was being lowered over him. What he said next surprised him nearly as much as it did Lucy. "I seen Bill Clements acting all eager-beaver when you two was at your locker a few times."

Color rose in Lucy's cheeks, a sign Zeke knew meant her temper was about to blow. "You can't mean that, Zeke. You know what kind of girl I am. Bill's in the marching band, as you well know, and we were talking about new formations and music for the halftime performance."

Lucy rubbed the spot between her eyes. When she looked at Zeke, it was as if all feeling had drained from her face. "You really are a jerk," she said. "Sounds to me like you did this to me, and now you're looking to pass the buck."

Zeke sat down and stared at his feet. A minute passed, and he looked at her. "What are you going to do?"

"You mean, what are *we* going to do?" Getting no reply, she said, "Okay, that's my first answer. I guess this is all on me. I've got one more year before I can graduate, which I want to do. I've worked too hard to throw that away. I'm about eight weeks in, I figure from what I found in that women's book in the town library. Another month or so, and I'll start showing."

Her fingers moved back and forth over the rough pine-plank seat. "You have no idea what this is going to do to me and my family. I'll have a bad reputation for the rest of my life. And this baby," she said and laid her hand on her stomach. "This baby, *our* baby, won't have a chance in this town."

Lucy stopped talking. Her eyes were dry, but her voice caught. "I swear, Zeke, a responsible guy wouldn't hesitate to —" She took a breath, and her shoulders shook. "Well," she said, "never mind."

Zeke thought about his football team, having a good old time right now. He had never felt so afraid. "Never mind what?"

"You need to be responsible, Zeke. It makes me sick I'm the one who has to say this." Lucy paused, then looked him straight in the eye. "What if we got married?"

Zeke felt the cage that had dropped on him earlier slam shut and lock. "I know you think I'm being chicken, Lucy, but I ain't. I just need time to think."

He kissed Lucy on the top of the head and turned to leave. When he got a few feet away, he looked back at her. She sat with her hands in her lap, staring ahead, looking at what, he didn't know.

Zeke didn't go to the party, and he didn't go to class the next day. At two in the afternoon, he showed up at Coach Benson's office and stuck his head through the open door. "Hey Coach, can I talk to you for a minute?"

Coach looked up and smiled. "Hey, Farrell. Sure, come on in. You look a little peaked. Too much celebrating last night?" He smiled and threw Zeke a wink.

"Yeah, something like that."

"So, what can I do for you?"

"What's my chances for getting a athletic scholarship at some college. Don't have to be the Razorbacks."

Coach held a rubber band hooked on his thumbs and tugged at either end. "Zeke, you've been one of my best players, and I'd say you're a shoo-in for All-District, but —"

His heart in his throat, Zeke managed, "But?"

"Zeke, your chances ain't good. Look, we're a small school in a small conference. But being one of my best players just won't cut it on the college level. You're not big enough or good enough to play college ball. Then there's your grades. You've barely got enough credits to graduate. You'd have trouble meeting college entrance requirements, and even if you did, you might not be eligible to play." Coach shook his head. "I'm not trying to bust your chops, Zeke. But that's the truth."

Zeke stood up, mumbled something the coach couldn't make out and left the office. He got in his old Chevy truck and headed toward the levees. After pondering as deep as he could into the afternoon, he drove back to school and waited till he saw Lucy heading toward her bus.

"You wanted me to be the responsible guy," Zeke shouted, eight months after his conversation with the coach. "When did that ever work out for me?"

Lucy took a step back from the clothesline where she was hanging Zeke's work clothes: dungarees, blue shirts with the gas station logo, underwear, socks. She took a wooden clothespin from her mouth and asked, "What are you talking about?"

Zeke was unsure on his feet, and he had that washed-out look he always got after he found somebody who'd sneak him a few beers. "Exactly what I said. I was the responsible guy on the football field, and it never got me nowhere. I was responsible at my job — when the boss decided to give the promotion I deserved to his no-account son — so that got me nothing. I stepped up and married you, and it didn't get me a kid or —"

Zeke saw their neighbor, old Mrs. Watkins, come into her backyard and stand near their adjoining fence. She looked ready to go to war. She looked like somebody who'd already won a few.

"You break my heart, Zeke, clean in two," Lucy said.

Lucy's eyes looked vacant, something Zeke had noticed more and more lately. The sight of her emptiness doused every bit of Zeke's anger, every word of his pitiful speech.

He walked over and put his arm around Lucy. "You know I didn't mean that. Say you know I didn't mean it."

Mrs. Watkins made some racket, running a stick across the rusted wire fence. Zeke continued. "Annie, ain't none of this is your fault. Losing the baby, the doctor telling you not to try to have no more. Them's just the cards we got dealt."

Zeke was crying then, and his tears seemed to appease Mrs. Watkins, who was now walking toward her back steps.

"I know I ain't worth a plug nickel sometimes, Lucy, but

I'll try to do better."

"I need you to do more than try, Zeke," Lucy said, and then she too turned and walked away.

It would be months before the sorrow in Lucy's eyes eased at all. In those weeks, Zeke straightened up. One Saturday near the end of May, he woke early and drove to the Donut Hut just to get Lucy a treat he thought would make her smile.

When he opened the box and showed her the donuts, some with colored sprinkles on top, she said, "I'm starting to believe you really do love me, Zeke Farrell."

Lucy grabbed two plates from the cabinet, and they sat side by side at the kitchen table. Zeke left his donut on the plate and took her hand. "I love you more than Christmas morning," he said.

"Let me ask you this. If you'd have gotten a football scholarship, would you have married me?"

Zeke blew out his breath. "Lucy, ever bit of hope I had rested on that danged game. I ain't the smartest fella, and it felt like football could've been my meal ticket." He realized he'd said it wrong. "I mean it could've been *our* meal ticket. When I lost that, it hit me in the gut." Talk of losing something he loved made him wince. Football didn't hold a candle to the baby they should have had.

He looked into her green eyes and remembered the way she'd looked on their first date, wearing a pink cardigan and a gray wool skirt. "But know this. Deep down, there weren't never a time I didn't want you by my side, honey, and that there's the God's honest truth."

Lucy didn't say a word, but she did scoot her chair closer to his. She did reach up and kiss his cheek.

Zeke knew he'd never forget that morning, the sun coming in through yellow gingham curtains. Lucy sitting at the table in her pink robe, and after they talked, eating donuts until they were full enough to bust. The birds of morning sang through the open window. When he closed his eyes and concentrated, he could hear them still.

# Chapter 21 — Preacher Jobe's Serpent

Jeb Compton wasn't a particularly religious man. He believed in God and had plenty of faith, but he didn't care much for all the trappings man had added on to the Bible. Truth be told, he felt closer to God in a deer stand than he did in church. That hadn't stopped his Annie. She'd dragged him to the First Baptist down on Elm Street almost every Sunday, but since her death, he'd not exactly been a regular.

"Hey, Homer. I met that new preacher fella for the Pentecostal church at the Walmart yesterday. I were stocking up on them fifty-pound bags of dog food 'cause you go through them like you got a hole in your belly. Anyways, he said he were going to have a surprise for his flock at the next service. I don't rightly know what to expect, but what say we head over there tonight and see what that be all about. Maybe do us some hunting later."

Homer, Jeb's big bluetick hound, sat gnawing on his ham bone, but he paused long enough to bark his agreement.

Preacher Jobe, a short, stout fellow with silver hair, bushy eyebrows, and a jutting chin, believed in what Mark 16:18 had to say about taking up serpents, but as he was fond of saying, "My ma didn't raise no fool." Mindful of that unfortunate episode with a cottonmouth at his last church in Kentucky, he'd traveled from Hurlin over to Little Rock. He needed to find a vet to remove Jezebel's venom glands. The large rattlesnake, a going-away present from a flock member, meant the world to him.

After getting a string of no's, and one Hell, no!, he was getting discouraged. Then Jesus guided him to the All Animal Veterinary Hospital on West Markham Street.

After hearing Jobe's request, Dr. Jim Liggett, a short, spare man with a horseshoe fringe of gray hair and a sour expression, eyed Jobe. "You know, this procedure is frowned upon by many herpetologists."

"I heard that, Doc, but —"

"In fact a veterinarian paper discouraged it for reasons of ethics and the animal's well-being."

"I can understand that Doc, but here's the thing: members of my congregation are going to be holding this old girl. They be safe enough if their faith is strong, of course, but if it ain't —"

Dr. Liggett pinched his thin lips together and frowned. He shook his head. "If those fools are going to be handling her, I suppose I have to do what I can to protect them."

"Thank you, Doc."

He wanted to add "Jesus bless you," but the look on the vet's stern face made Jobe think he might not take kindly to it. He mouthed it silently instead.

After the operation and recovery time, Jobe settled up with the vet. He took Jezebel to his old '65 Ford pick-up truck and placed her cage in the cab. "Don't take it personal, old girl." Jezebel lay coiled in her cage and stared at him with cold reptilian eyes.

"I just think surely Jesus don't want me to take no chances. Of course, the flock don't need to know you've been worked on. When they hold you, they need to believe they're proving their faith."

Reaching the Hurlin city limits sign, newly decorated with a couple of .22 bullet holes, he pulled into the church's gravel parking lot. He set the parking brake and admired the sign. Beneath the Church of Jesus Pentecostal name, he read, Today's To-Do List: Thank Jesus! "Amen to that, Jezebel," Preacher Jobe said.

The sign was new enough, but the old forty-by-sixty-foot building could use some sprucing up. Someone had told the preacher it was built in the thirties by the Public Works Administration as part of that Roosevelt fella's New Deal. It had been a city hall, then a post office, a general store, and finally a church. The native fieldstone walls looked to be holding up well enough, but the oak wood steeple could use some boards replaced. A new coat of white paint wouldn't hurt either, and the roof could use some new shingles. Preacher Jobe would have to have a talk with the finance committee to see what was possible.

He turned his attention to the snake. "Well, Jezebel," he said, "the Lord will provide, but maybe you and me can stir up some help tonight in the offerings department." He got out and removed her cage. He entered the church, carrying

Jezebel, and stopped to pet the orange church cat curled up on a pew, who hissed at the serpent. For the next hour or so, he practiced his sermon in the church's back room while Jezebel rested.

The evening service started at 7:00 p.m. Cars and trucks commenced filling up the parking lot thirty minutes before. Preacher Jobe stood by the double church doors and greeted folk as they approached.

Jeb Compton stepped up. "Evening, Preacher."

"Evening, Jeb. Glad you could make it. I see you've got your hound in the back of your truck. Is he a bluetick?"

"Yes, sir, he be. I'm going coon hunting after the service, and I brung old Homer with to save a trip back to the house. Don't worry none; I've got him tied up with a rope."

"He ain't going to howl during the service, is he?"

"Nah. He'll most likely settle down and take him a nap till we're done."

"Well, then. Good to see you again. Find you a seat you fancy."

"I'll do that. You going to leave them doors open?"

Preacher Jobe laughed. "On a hot, sticky night like this? Count on it. I've already shucked my jacket."

Jeb entered and found him a seat near the back, and soon the two rows of pews were filling up with folks. The service proceeded in fine fashion with plenty of loud praying, singing, and clapping. Halfway through the song part of the service, Ella Bagwell, the spinster town librarian, caught the Holy Ghost. She jumped to her feet with her arms thrust up. Her eyes rolled back in her head. She started speaking in tongues. Her words sounded like a different language, or maybe four or five foreign languages put together. The rest of the flock looked mighty impressed, especially after she fainted dead away. Jeb waited for an interpreter to explain

what she'd said since he'd heard that's how these things
went, but no one stood up to offer any explanation. After
Miss Ella revived and was helped back to her seat, she fanned
herself with her hand fan from the local funeral home and
looked, it seemed to Jeb, proud as punch.

Next, the Holy Ghost grabbed hold of Sam Spencer. Sam,
a tall, stocky man with a red beard and a smug expression,
wore an ill-fitting suit and tie. He dropped to the floor,
thrashing and rolling around. He bumped into several flock
members and ended up under the old grand piano. When he
snapped out of it, he stood and brushed the dust off his suit.
He adjusted his tie, stiffly returned to his seat, and tried to
look casual-like, as if nothing had transpired.

Preacher Jobe called for quiet, and the flock subsided. "I
want to introduce y'all to someone. Now, y'all ain't used to
seeing such, I know, but we did this all the time back at my
last church."

After the preacher prayed, he opened his worn Bible,
licked his finger, and flipped the satiny pages until he came
across the scripture he wanted. "It says here in the Book of
Mark, 'They shall take up serpents; and if they drink any
deadly thing, it shall not hurt them; they shall lay hands on
the sick, and they shall recover.'

"And we do believe the Word, don't we?" He sounded like
a carny at the state fair to Jeb, one who was asking questions
that were sure to lead to trouble. Still, several of the flock
said, "Amen, Preacher!"

Jeb crossed his arms. He was thinking of how he'd kept it
mowed around his pond, the fear he had that Homer would
come across a water moccasin when he was splashing
around. A shiver went down his back.

Just then, Preacher Jobe bent over, pulled the cloth off the
cage sitting by him on the floor, and carefully removed

Jezebel. She was a big snake, brown with a diamond pattern across her body, and the noise-making rattler at the end of her tail might have been heard had not the entire congregation been gasping.

The preacher held the snake with both hands, and slowly raised his arms above his head. The growing murmurs of the congregation were peppered with comments like, "Look at the size of that thing!" And then a woman near the back screamed. And another exited through the open doors, her high heels clacking across the floor.

"Settle down," Preacher Jobe said. "This here be Jezebel, and as you can tell, I have not one ounce of fear holding her. She is the very incarnation of a demon, true enough, but the Lord Jesus gave us dominion over such."

He paused, it seemed to Jeb, to ramp up the drama even more.

When he spoke, he said, "Who among you will come up here and hold this poison viper to test your faith?"

Folks snuck a peek at their neighbors. The muttering grew louder still. A few congregants elbowed the ones next to them. The words, "I dare you," were heard.

As for Jeb, he wondered what he'd gotten himself into. At about the same time, Homer, from his perch in the back of Jeb's truck, spied the church cat on the steps. He lunged forward, the rope snapped, and he leaped off of the truck bed and barreled toward the cat. When the orange feline saw him coming, she hightailed it through the open church doors. Homer, howling like a banshee, tore down the aisle after the cat.

Trying to shake Homer, the cat veered to the right, sprang on top the grand piano, ran down the keys, and doubled back. She darted between Preacher Jobe's legs, and Homer followed. The good man got knocked cattywampus by the sixty-pound dog and staggered against the pulpit. The sanctified preacher flung his arms out for balance, and the rattlesnake Jezebel sailed through the air, landing in the lap of Bertie Mae Johnson.

Likely outraged by her unplanned flight, Jezebel sank her fangs in one of Bertie Mae's meaty thighs. Bertie let out a whoop, jumped so high in the air that she nearly touched the ceiling, and somehow landed her ample frame on the seat of the pew. It was a feat that was remarked upon for weeks afterward.

Jezebel was again launched. The air-born rattler landed in the aisle, and the entire congregation clambered over the backs of the pews, climbed over each other, or ran so fast their feet barely hit the floor. It seemed to Jeb that the church emptied faster than the weak bladder of a dedicated beer drinker.

In the aftermath, Preacher Jobe found Jezebel, picked her up carefully, and put her in her cage. Jeb corralled Homer, promising the hound a stick of deer jerky he just happened to have in his back pocket. Bertie Mae, who'd lost a good fifty pounds since taking her job as a taste-tester, was slim enough to fit in Sister Goodson's little Datson, but just barely, and they sped away to see Doc Wilkens. No one seemed to know what became of the cat.

The next Sunday, the church was nearly empty, even though the preacher had the good sense to leave Jezebel at home. But in the weeks to come, a few stragglers came in, and then a few more, and, finally the bulk of the congregation returned, bringing others with them. The pews filled, as did the collection plates.

They hadn't come to see Jezebel. No, they were done with that business. They had shown up with the hopes of seeing Sister Bertie Mae Johnson, who had been struck by that demon serpent and lived to tell about it. Praise be to God.

The next time Jeb drove past the church, he took note of the sign. It read, The Lord Jesus works in mysterious ways.

Jeb looked at Homer, who was sitting next to him and said, "He sure do, Homer. He surely do."

# Chapter 22 — Nudging The Hereafter

Jeb Compton hiked up his flannel shirt and rubbed Ben-Gay on his aching lower back. He looked at his big bluetick hound, who wrinkled up his muzzle and sneezed. "Not taking kindly to the smell, eh, Homer? It are a mite intense, but it sure do the trick when I get sore from bouncing around on that old tractor all day." Homer looked doubtful and kept his distance. "Used to not need it so much, but age takes a toll on a man. On a dog, too. You'll find that out for your ownself one day." Jeb rubbed his chin. "But I needn't complain. I'm sure older folk than me got it worse. Our neighbor, Jake, is getting up there. I never heard him go on about his aches and pains, and I'm sure he suffers worse than me."

At the ripe old age of seventy-five, Jake Byer finally understood the Law of Diminishing Returns. Everything he tried these days kept him barely even or backsliding by degrees. Jake had always held his own in a fair fight, but old age didn't play that tune. It trotted out weapons like arthritis and glaucoma. It plagued him with diminishing short-term memory and loss of balance. It saddled him with hardening of the arteries and high blood pressure.

Jake sat in an Adirondack chair, fashioned by his grandfather, on his old porch, the planks of which were formed of weathered oak. He looked over at the crazy patchwork quilt that covered Roy, his Catahoula Leopard Dog. "You know how it is, don't you, boy? Life is a continuing investment, but it's getting harder making the blamed payments."

The ninety-pound hound lifted his head off the porch and peered at Jake through eyes that held piercing black pupils floating in a sea of milky-blue irises. Roy seemed to ponder the question, then became distracted by a cottontail venturing out of a nearby field.

Seeing this, Jake shook his head. "Yeah, boy, I'll bet chasing that rabbit appeals to you more than keeping me company. Why don't you go get him?"

Roy hesitated, switching his gaze back and forth between Jake and the rabbit. The rabbit won out, and Jake found himself alone on the porch.

Ain't no big thing, he thought. Being alone was a state he'd been visiting more and more over time. Since most of his old friends had died, and his Emmy Lou had joined them a few years back, he'd had a good while to get used to it. Most times, Roy and the chores provided enough distraction. The nighttime, though, was another matter. Sometimes the silence, punctured only by the calls of the tree frogs and the hoots of a great horned owl nesting in his big sycamore tree, weighed heavily on him.

The sound of a car crunching the gravel in his driveway caught his attention. A blue Ford Fairlane ground to a halt, and Jake's daughter emerged. Brenda, a pleasant-looking woman of forty-five, with Jake's green eyes and Emmy Lou's black hair, gazed over the old homestead, then zeroed in on Jake.

"Hi, Daddy," she said. "Hey, I don't see Roy. What's he up to?"

"Hi, baby girl. Last I saw him, he had an appointment with a rabbit. I reckon he'll be back when it's time for lunch. So, what brings you out to these parts?"

Brenda came over and bent to give her father a hug and a peck on his stubbled cheek. "Just wanted to check in on my daddy. See how he's doing."

Jake smiled. "Hanging in there, pretty lady. Like a hair on a biscuit." He pulled out a handkerchief and mopped his forehead. "This humidity is sure something else. It's like sucking air through a wet dishrag."

"Or, sucking molasses through a straw," she said.

Jake grinned. They'd played this "one-upmanship" game since Brenda was a little girl, and he loved that she'd discovered on the joy of language through their verbal sparring. "Or, coaxing a camel through the eye of a needle."

Brenda laughed. "I never could beat you at that, but I loved trying. Those were fun times."

He smiled. "Yes, they were."

"Hey, why don't you come with me over to the car?" Brenda said, changing the subject. "Got something I want to show you."

Jake started to rise, but a sudden wrenching pain in his lower back made him grunt and fall back into his chair.

Brenda's eyes looked enormous. "What's wrong, Daddy?"

Jake gritted his teeth and waved away her question. "It ain't nothing, Daughter. Just tweaked my back some taking those bags of chicken feed off the truck. I'll lay on a hot water bottle tonight, and it will be right as rain by tomorrow."

Brenda didn't appear convinced. "You've got to be more careful, Daddy. You know you're not as young as you used to be."

Jake snorted. "Ain't no one as young as they used to be, Honey."

"But —"

Jake made a slashing movement with his right hand. "That's enough, now. I said it will be fine."

Brenda bowed up. "Daddy, I'm not a little girl anymore, and you're not going to buffalo me like you used to. I think we need to go see the doctor. I'm worried about you."

Jake's eyes flashed like sparklers on the Fourth of July, but he tamped down his temper. "Didn't mean to snap at you. If it ain't better by tomorrow, I'll run by the clinic and have them take a look-see. How's that?"

Brenda nodded. "Okay, then. Listen, you just sit there, and I'll get what I wanted to show you from the car." A minute later, she returned with some brochures.

Jake pointed a finger at them. "What are those?"

"These are from some of the retirement homes around here. I wanted you to see what all they have to offer."

Jake stared at her. "What in Sam Hill are you talking about? I ain't going to no retirement home."

Brenda flinched but stood her ground. "I'm not saying it has to be right now, Daddy, but when the time comes, I want to be ready."

Despite the pain, Jake stood. "Brenda, I said I ain't going.

Not now. Not later. It ain't happening. I've lived on this land all my life, as my daddy did before me, and his daddy before him. This is Byers' land and will be as long as I've got anything to say about it. One day, if you want it, it will be yours."

Tears trickled down Brenda's cheeks. "Why are you so stubborn? I'm just trying to look out for you." When Jake didn't reply, she continued. "Can you honestly tell me you're not finding it harder to keep going like you used to?" Jake remained silent, and Brenda stamped her foot. "Daddy, be truthful with me, please."

The "please" nailed Jake between his eyes. He carefully eased himself back down into his chair and looked up at her. "Of course, it's getting harder. I'd be lying if I tried to say otherwise. But can't you try seeing things from my side? I've lived here my whole life. Pastor Brown married your mother and me in the living room of this house, and your mother bore you in our bedroom. This house saw you through chicken pox and the flu. It witnessed you through eighteen birthdays, and then bringing that young man of yours home to meet us. I couldn't leave this place. All the wonderful things that God has blessed me with happened right here. I couldn't bear to go and, when my time comes, I want it to be here."

Brenda broke down, sinking slowly to the porch beside her father's chair. Jake smoothed her hair with one calloused hand and waited till her sobs subsided. "It will be all right, Honey."

"Will it, Daddy? Will it?"

"I believe that, Daughter, as sure as I believe the sun will rise tomorrow."

"And if it's not?"

Jake thought about it. "Then, I reckon it will be in God's

hands and out of mine."

"Okay, Daddy. Let's leave it at that for now. Just remember, I'm only a phone call away if you need me."

"I know. Now you'd best be getting home to that husband and younguns of yours."

Brenda stood and hugged Jake's neck. She frowned at the brochures. "What should I do with these?"

"Tell you what." Jake said and offered her a weary smile. "Why don't you leave them with me? It won't hurt me none to take a look-see, just in case things don't work out like I want them to."

Beaming a smile that could pierce the cloudiest Arkansas day, Brenda headed for her car. When she drove out of sight, Jake spread the shiny pamphlets across his lap. There was a falseness to the happy photos showing old folks laughing too hard over a game of cards, or sitting like schoolchildren around laminate tables in a too-bright dining hall.

He could not imagine himself there, no Roy at his side, the land he'd loved all his life so far away he couldn't smell the living dirt of it, or see the yellow Coreopsis flowers climbing across the hill each spring. But what did he owe the land, he wondered, and what did he owe his only daughter, who broke into tears at the sorry sight of him?

Jake stacked the brochures just so on the arm of his chair. He rubbed his chin and said aloud, "I'm so old, the alarm bell goes off when I try to leave a museum."

He listened, halfway wishing he'd hear one of his good buddies try to one-up him. When no one answered, he called for Roy, his last true friend. He painfully stood, waiting for the old boy to come on home.

## Chapter 23 — A Nice Tip

The large bluetick hound poked his head out of the tall field grass that edged the garden and spied Jeb sitting on the porch, reading. He made a beeline over, bounded up the steps, shoved the newspaper aside, and plopped his head in Jeb's lap. "Dang it, Homer, get off. You're all wet. And what's that on your face and ears? Cobwebs? You be a mess, and now you be making me one, too."

Jeb grabbed a towel from the kitchen and worked Homer over. "I were looking in the paper and seen an ad for the Dixie Diner. That got me thinking on how I miss my Annie's cooking and how I be getting real tired of my own. They do ham and eggs up right. Them biscuits of theirs is real flaky too, and their coffee's a sight better than mine. I'll fetch you back some leftovers. How do that strike you?"

Homer barked, and Jeb laughed. "All right, then. If I leave

now, they still be time to tend them soybeans. Try to stay out of trouble."

Jeb fired up his old Ford truck and headed to downtown Hurlin. As he turned right off Main Street, he could see the diner sign a few blocks ahead. A Hurlin landmark, the sign was an ancient '53 Chevy Rat Rod truck welded atop a twelve-foot steel column. Dixie Diner, in bright yellow script, decorated the faded black doors on either side. He pulled in and parked.

Jeb picked out a wooden peg on the wall near the front door, hung up his jacket, and found a corner booth. After delivering a meal to a nearby table, Sally Lowery came over. "Mr. Compton, it's been ages. How are you?"

"I'm okay, Miss Sally. Good to see you again."

Sally's smile slipped a notch. "I was sure sorry to hear about Annie. I loved that woman to pieces."

"Thank you. And the same goes for me with your grandma. She were a special lady, and I miss talking to her. How you holding up?"

Sally teared up. "It's hard. Guess I don't need to tell you that."

Jeb's eyes felt moist. "No, ma'am."

"Ain't we a fine pair, then."

Jeb nodded. "That we is."

Sally sighed. "Well, anyway, what are you drinking?"

"Coffee, please. Black."

"Coming right up. You know what you want to eat, or do you need me to grab you a menu?"

"Two fried eggs, over easy, a slice of ham, some biscuits and gravy, and a side order of hash."

Sally turned to the cut-out kitchen window behind the counter. "Hey, Sam, I need two cackle fruit, flop 'em, a Noah's boy, heart attack on rack, and mystery in the alley."

Jeb stared at Sally. "Say what, now?"

Sally turned and gave Jeb a sly grin. "Just giving the cook your order."

"That were my order?"

"Well, yes, in waitress-speak. I'll go get that coffee."

While he waited for his breakfast, Jeb took in his surroundings — framed pictures of singers and personalities, some of them signed, decorated the knotty pine paneling on the walls; a mounted large-mouth bass, in the eight-pound range — lorded over all from above the kitchen window; a Formica table with six chairs hosted a group of the regulars, who were talking over each other.

Jeb saw a few familiar faces as they swapped political views, stories, and outright lies. One new face, a beefy-looking fella in grease-stained work clothes, held forth loudly and often in a strident voice, accompanied by wild arm gestures.

Sally returned with Jeb's food. He thanked her and said, "You know, I got to know your grandma pretty well, but I never did meet your grandpa. I were always kind of curious 'bout him. She didn't bring him up much, as I recall."

Sally laughed. "No doubt, she didn't. Grandpa Earl, according to my mom, provided Grandma a steady dose of aggravation. Folks around here called him 'Turtle Earl.'"

Jeb raised an eyebrow. "He were that Earl? He be a legend in these parts."

"Yep. One and the same. The Depression hit folks hard, Mom said. They were always worried about their next meal, and Grandpa Earl caught all kinds of turtles for soup: snappers, softshells, red-eared sliders. If it had a shell, Grandpa Earl caught it."

"I'll be danged."

Sally's eyes held a mischievous sparkle. "You knew

Grandma held her religion dear?"

Jeb smiled. "Yes. We talked the ins-and-outs of that subject on several occasions."

"Well, apparently Grandpa Earl took another view. Mom said that man didn't have a drop of pretension in him and didn't care much for those who did. To his mind, that included the Baptist ladies from Grandma's Bible study group. 'Bunch of holier than thous,' he called them. Well, one Sunday after church, they came by to visit Grandma. They were all gussied up in their Sunday best, and each one carried a Bible.

"While they were chatting with Grandma out in the yard, Grandpa Earl disappeared into the shed. When he came back out, he carried a big copper pot and a short iron rod. He commenced banging on that pot and singing "Will the Circle Be Unbroken" at the top of his lungs. After those ladies got over their shock, their noses went so high in the air they could have snagged them on a tree branch. They didn't hang around long after that. Grandpa Earl pulled a lot of stunts and stayed in Grandma's doghouse a good part of the time."

Jeb laughed till he had to grab his napkin to wipe his eyes. "That right there be a great tale. I believe I'd a liked that fella."

"From what Mom told me, a lot of folks did. Now you best get to eating before your breakfast gets cold."

Sally left to tend to another table. Jeb ate, savoring the taste of the pan-fried brown sugar ham and the peppery zing of the sausage gravy over the flaky buttermilk biscuits. That cook deserves him a raise, he thought.

A commotion shattered the enjoyment of his meal. He looked toward the source. The beefy fella he'd noted earlier pushed his chair back and jumped up. A large, wet stain covered the front of his shirt. Red-faced and trembling, he yelled at Sally. "You dumb heifer. You spilled hot coffee on me."

Sally's face drained of color. "I'm sorry, Mister, but you bumped my arm as I was putting down your cup."

The man's voice grew louder. "Oh, so you're saying this was my fault?"

"I'm not saying that, no. It was an accident."

"Accident, my rear. They ought to fire you and find somebody that can do your job. And that's what they'll do if I got anything to say about it."

Stony-faced, Jeb laid down his knife and fork. He walked over to the table and tapped the man on the shoulder. The man wheeled around. "What do you want?"

"I want you to back off. That is no way to be treating a lady."

The man's eyes bulged, and his face purpled. "Lady? Her? Why she ain't nothing but a no-account —"

Jeb's voice cut through like a serrated knife. "That's enough! I said back off, and I mean just that."

The man kicked back his chair and swung a wild haymaker at Jeb's head. Before it could connect, Jeb clamped the man's arm in an iron grip and wrenched it behind his back. He howled in pain.

Jeb frog-marched the man across the diner and out the door.

A few minutes later, he returned and approached a clearly shaken Sally who sat at an empty table. "He'll not be back anytime soon. You okay?"

"Yes, I think so. It really was an accident, you know?"

"Accident or no, he had no business talking at you like that."

"That was really something; I've never seen the like. Where did you learn to fight like that?"

"I were in World War II. Before they shipped us overseas, I done a stint as a MP. We was taught how to deal with drunks and such. Guess the training ain't completely wore off, but I'm sorry you had to see that."

"Are you kidding me? That was amazing. Thank you so much for what you did."

Jeb's ears reddened. "You is welcome. Now I need to be getting back to my breakfast. If you get a chance, could you bring me something to put them leftovers in? I got a hungry hound that won't be none too happy if I'm gone too long. Oh, wait —" Jeb dug in his pocket, fished out three dollar bills, and handed them to Sally. "This is for his meal. He asked me to give it to you."

Sally looked at the money. "But that's way too much."

"Well, he insisted you get a nice tip." He threw Sally a wink and headed back to his booth.

# Chapter 24 — Predator

Jeb Compton took an oatmeal cookie from the stack on the plate that Sadie Thompson had brought by. He took a bite and slowly chewed, savoring the taste of the added raisins. Right nice, he thought.

A pitiful whine interrupted his enjoyment, and he looked down from his porch chair at his bluetick hound sitting beside him. "Homer, I swear I ain't never seen a sadder expression on a dog's face. Didn't I just feed you a little while back?"

Eyes glued to the cookie Jeb held, Homer ignored the reminder and seemed to do his best to look even more mournful.

Jeb chuckled. "Okay, you done convinced me that you be starving to death. Here you go."

Homer snagged the tidbit out of mid-air, swallowed it

with one gulp, and looked at Jeb. "That be it, dog. These be too good to waste on someone who don't even chew."

Jeb leaned back in his chair and licked his fingers. "You know, Homer, Sadie's the third lady to stop by this past week and bring me something to eat. First, it were Bertie Mae Johnson with that casserole. Then Ella Johnson with them muffins. I can understand that happening in the days after Annie passed, but that be thirteen months ago now. I wonder what this is all about; it's a head-scratcher for sure. Oh well, we can't look a gift horse in the mouth, can we?"

Betsy Chandler shaved her legs, combed her long black hair, stuffed herself into her girdle, and slipped on her dress. In her youth, she wouldn't have needed the undergarment. She'd just sashay her hips and men would come running. Danged Father Time sure didn't do women no favors. Now, at forty, she had to use every trick in her arsenal. Of course, she didn't have to go hunting for a husband. The previous three had left her well enough off, but the thought of being without a husband didn't sit right.

Betsy tugged at the fabric of her dress, smoothing it across her hips. She turned her head sideways, looked in the full-length mirror, and nodded approvingly. Still plenty good enough for the job at hand.

Pickings had been slim in the Hurlin area this past year, but a new prospect joined the list of possibilities when Jeb Compton became a widower. Betsy didn't figure him for a cash cow, but he did cut a fine figure as a man, and right now, she needed the comfort of a good-looking man. She'd given him enough time to get over the worst of the grieving, at least in her book. Of course, she knew the town's heifers would be thinking the same way, and come sniffing around. But those women clearly didn't measure up. They didn't call her the "man-eater" for nothing.

Betsy went to the carport and unlocked her '70 Buick Skylark. Before climbing in, she stepped back a few paces to admire the vehicle, a birthday gift from her last husband, Frank. The black pin-striping really accented the car's hot pink paint.

Too bad old Frank committed suicide after the bank discovered he'd embezzled, she thought. She'd just about worked him around to taking her on a trip to Cancun.

On the way through town, she stopped at Myrtie Mae's Bakery and picked out a nice-looking apple pie. She continued down Highway 49 and turned down the lane to Jeb Compton's house. Seeing Jeb sitting on the porch with his hound, she parked her car, took the pie out of its container, and sashayed toward him.

Her presentation came to an abrupt halt as a sixty-pound behemoth barreled over, reared up, and planted two huge paws on her shoulders. She staggered back and went down on her bottom. The pie fared no better; it flew through the air and hit the ground top-down. Jeb came running over to get Homer, but the hound had already abandoned Betsy and stood devouring the pie's remains.

Jeb helped Betsy to her feet. "Is you all right, Mrs. Chandler?"

Betsy brushed off her rear. "I think so. I was just so frightened."

She glanced at Homer and tried not to smile as inspiration struck. She worked up a tear or two and said, "And look at the pie. I spent all morning baking that, and now it's ruined."

Jeb hung his head. "I'm so sorry, Mrs. Chandler. If I'd a

knowed you were coming by, I would a tied Homer up. Please, come up on the porch and sit a spell."

"Why, thank you. And call me Betsy, please." Jeb saw Betsy to a chair and went to the kitchen to get her a glass of lemonade. Betsy sat down, wincing as her bottom made contact with the wooden seat. Jeb returned with a glass and handed it to her. She made sure to lean forward when she took it so he could get him a peep. She smiled and took a swallow, and her green eyes bulged as the sugar intensity hit her.

He looked concerned. "Is it too sweet for you?"

She forced herself to take another drink. "Why, no. It's perfect."

"That's good. My dear Annie always claimed I had a sweet tooth. Glad someone else shares my taste."

That sweet tooth of his is one of the first things that has to change, she thought. She looked over at Homer as he finished off the pie. And there's another.

Jeb took a seat. "So, Betsy, what brings you by on this fine day?"

"Oh, someone mentioned you the other day, and I realized I hadn't seen you around lately. I thought I'd come over and see how you were doing." She looked down at her glass. "With Frank gone, the good Lord rest his soul, it's been kind of lonesome, and I thought it would be nice to talk to someone who knows what that's like."

"Well, I were sure sorry to hear about Frank, and I surely do know what you been going through. It's right hard."

Betsy placed her hand over his. "I knew you'd understand." Jeb's ears reddened. He pulled his hand away like he'd set it on a hot stove, then stared at it as if he'd never seen it before. Oops, Betsy thought, it's too soon, and in this game timing is everything. "Oh, Jeb, I'm sorry. I didn't mean to —"

Jeb found his voice with a quaver attached. "No. It ain't your fault. You just caught me by surprise. I know you didn't mean nothing by it."

Jeb was so rusty he didn't know he was being flirted with, she thought. Not the smartest man, but that's okay; I'm not after him for his brains. Still, he looks uncomfortable, so a distraction might be order. She smiled. "So, how are your crops coming along?"

"They be doing real good right now. I got a couple of acres at the bottom of the field that was stunted. I couldn't figure out what were causing it, but I called the County Extension agent, and he got right to the solution. Turns out drainage were the problem."

Betsy fidgeted in her chair.

"Yes, sir, it seems like all them cattails and grass in the ditch was catching leaves and branches and such, and the irrigation water couldn't drain. After I cleaned out them ditches, things got better."

Dear God, make him stop, Betsy thought.

"Course, now I got to worry about them stink bugs showing up. They can ruin a crop right quick if they ain't controlled. And I been thinking a trying this new type of fertilizer they recommend. Not them stink bugs, of course, them can't recommend nothing, but the co-op surely can. I suppose —"

Betsy jumped to her feet. "Oh, my goodness, Jeb, look at the time. I just remembered I have an appointment at the bank. I'd better get going."

"That's too bad. I had me some other things we could talk on."

Betsy was off the porch and headed to her car when she turned around. "I'm real sorry, Jeb, but I have to make this appointment. Another time, maybe?"

Jeb smiled. "Sure thing. Come by anytime." He watched Betsy hightail it down the lane, then turned and walked to the kitchen. Homer accompanied him while licking pie crumbs off his muzzle. Jeb picked up the handset on the rotary phone, dialed the number of the Dixie Diner, and asked for Sally Lowery.

"Howdy, Sally, this is Jeb Compton. I won't keep you, but I wanted to let you know that Betsy Chandler come by to see me. Yeah, it were just like you warned me about, but Homer and me dealt with her. I don't 'spect I'll be seeing her again no time soon. Thanks again for tipping me off."

After Jeb hung up the phone, he looked down at his hound. "Good job, Homer. Danged shame about that pie, though."

## Chapter 25 — Getting By

Jeb Compton, accompanied by his hound, Homer, strolled down the country lane leading from his house to the main road. They stopped to watch a covey of bobwhite quail scoot across their path. While watching, Jeb kept a hand on Homer's collar in case the hound was tempted to do more than watch.

"We could of hopped in my truck and been here quicker, Homer, but it be a nice morning, I needed to stretch my legs, and I love to watch them quail."

He'd just finished speaking when a spooked cottontail bolted from his cover and shot across the lane. Homer looked at Jeb and whined.

"Okay Homer, go get him."

He didn't need to tell the hound twice. Jeb continued on till he reached his rusting mailbox with its missing door. As he retrieved his morning mail, he spoke to his hound, then realized he addressed empty air. The mailbox was a pitiful sight, and it needed replacing. "She's sure seen better days," Jeb said out loud, "but I reckon she ain't alone in that."

He spotted a small dust cloud in the distance, heading down the road in his direction. The cloud grew larger as the vehicle approached, and Jeb could soon make out a powder blue AMC Rambler Classic bouncing down the road. As it drew near, the driver slowed. When she passed by, she waved. Jeb caught a snatch of Johnny Cash's gravelly voice rasping out "A Boy Named Sue" on the radio. He'd seen the Man in Black once at the Hurlin Fair some years back, and Jeb could picture him on stage, singing and strumming the neck of his guitar.

The driver was Tracy Scoggins, Jeb believed, probably on her way to visit her aunt Martha who lived down the road a ways.

The car lived up to its name, Tracy Scoggins thought, as it rambled along the twisting dirt road. She replayed the scene at the used car lot in her mind. The salesman had gone on and on about the car. "Yes, ma'am, she may not look that classy, but she's super reliable, easy to handle, and the price is a lot less than them other brands — only $2,098 when new." He flashed a smile. "Of course, with a hundred thousand miles on the odometer, we've come down some from that.

"She's not like them foreign jobs, neither," he continued. "They made her from good old American steel in Kenosha, Wisconsin, U.S. of A. She's got her a V8 engine, 250 cubic inches, with a die-cast block that has iron alloy cylinders and produces 127.5 horsepower." He smacked the hood with an open palm, making Tracy jump. "Yep. Just old-fashioned American quality found here. Heck, folks like it so much, they took to calling her the Kenosha Cadillac. Ain't that something?"

Tracy bought it because she liked the color, and she couldn't afford more. She mentally crossed her fingers as she paid for it and hoped for the best.

The car gave a lurch as it hit yet another rut. Kenosha Cadillac, my rear, thought Tracy. More like the Wisconsin Woebegone. Just then, she turned down the lane leading to her aunt's place and pulled to a stop in the gravel driveway.

Exiting her car, she crunched over to the porch, clomped up the wooden stairs, and rapped on the door jamb.

A minute later, Martha Basham pulled the door open, pushed out the screen door, and smiled at her niece. "Tracy, it's good to see you, child. Come on in and set a spell."

Once inside, Martha plopped down in her old cane rocker and motioned her niece to take a seat on a flowery-print sofa. Tracy sank into the soft cushion, then leaned back.

"You're looking fit as a fiddle, child. I'm thinking life must be agreeing with you."

Tracy smiled, which emphasized the dimples in her cheeks. "I'd have to say so, yes. School's going well, I've got a part-time job as a teller at the First National Bank, and —"

Martha hoisted an eyebrow. "And?"

Tracy's smile lit up her face like a fireworks display on the Fourth of July. She held out her left hand to show off the gold ring with a cluster of small diamonds. "Aunt Martha, I'm engaged!"

Martha made a big to-do over the ring, then she asked, "Who's the lucky fellow?"

"His name's Joe Conklin. He's one year up on me in

college, majors in business, and plays center field for the baseball team on a scholarship. He's got big plans for the future, and he wants them to include me."

Martha nodded. "Sounds like quite a catch. Course he's getting one, too, if you ask me."

Tracy blushed. "Thanks, Aunt Martha." Her smile, so radiant when talking about her fiancé, slipped a notch. "But how about you? Are you doing okay?"

Martha cocked her head. "Me? I'm doing just fine, child. Why wouldn't I be?"

A touch of sadness clouded Tracy's hazel eyes. "I worry about you, that's all. Here all by yourself. Doesn't it ever get lonely? You're not even sixty yet. Don't you ever think about maybe getting married again?"

A sneer hiked up the left corner of Martha's mouth, but her brown eyes sparkled with good humor. "Me? Get hitched again? Honey, let me tell you something. At my age, there are only two kinds of men interested in me: ones ailing and wanting someone to take care of them, and ones down on their luck and wanting a crack at my money." She grinned. "Well, I'm here to tell you, I ain't going to be a nurse or a purse for no man."

Tracy chuckled. "You'll never change, Aunt Martha."

"Not likely, child. Not likely. But don't you fret over it. I've got my garden to tend to, my chickens to care for, and my books and records to keep me company. Fact is, I'm happy as a hog in slop. Now, tell me some more about that fellow of yours."

After Tracy happily gushed for a few minutes — with time out for sweet tea and sugar cookies. At some point, Tracy glanced at her watch and said, "My, look at the time. I've got to get moving. There's a hundred things I need to be doing."

Martha smiled and stood up. "I'll bet. Thanks so much for

dropping by. I know it's a far piece. Now, come give your aunt a big hug, and then skedaddle. And next time bring that beau of yours."

After watching her niece depart, Martha returned to her rocker and sat down with a grunt. Well, she thought, that was a heck of a performance if I do say so. Should get me some kind of acting award — maybe one of them Oscars.

Her eyes wandered the room, stopping when they reached the pictures on the oak mantle over the stone fireplace. Her eyes fastened on her wedding picture, and she addressed her husband. "Oh, James, I miss you something fierce. Not a day goes by I don't think of you. I know you never approved my telling whoppers, but I couldn't tell the child the truth — how sometimes the loneliness just eats at me to the point where I'm ready to join you."

Martha rubbed away a tear that couldn't be contained. Enough of such things, she thought. I need to get my head on straight and tend to things that need tending. She stood up, went to the kitchen, and grabbed her address book off the counter. After leafing through it till she found the number she wanted, she picked up the handset of her phone and dialed.

"Jeb here."

"Hey, Jeb, this is Martha Basham."

"Howdy, Martha. Good to hear from you. What's up?"

"I've got me some shingles in need of replacing, and I seem to recollect you telling me once that you knew a good roofer."

"Sure do. Leastways, he done a fine job for Annie and me. Right reasonable, too. Hold on a minute, and I'll see if I still got his business card." When Jeb returned with the information, she wrote down the number and thanked him.

After scheduling an appointment with the roofer for the

next morning, she fed the chickens and gathered eggs. She made supper and afterward decided to turn in early. As she was shutting down the house for the night, she picked up her wedding picture one more time, marveling at how young she and James looked. Martha kissed the underside of her forefinger and put it against the image of his young face. "Night, darling. Love you."

# CHAPTER 26 — AND MORE

A dusty brown Chevy panel truck with a ladder strapped to the roof bounced down her lane and pulled to a stop. Martha saw the dark brown lettering on the door proclaiming *Brown's Roofing & More.* She shook her head. That man does like his brown, she thought.

A tall, spare man of her approximate age stepped down from his cab. He had rippling brown hair that was just beginning to gray at the temples, and it reminded her of a series of waves on the surface of the ocean. He came over to the porch, stuck out his hand, and said, "Hello, ma'am. I'm Paul."

Martha cut him off with a grin. "Let me guess: Paul Brown."

Paul returned a sly smile. "Actually, ma'am, it's Paul White. Brown was the fellow I bought the rig from when he decided to retire. The lettering is so pretty; I didn't have the heart to change it."

Martha laughed and shook his hand, approving of his firm grip. "Howdy, Paul. I'm Martha, and I've got some shingles in need of replacing. Time was I'd have done it myself, but I ain't a spring chicken no more."

Paul's eyebrows shot up. "You did roofing?"

"What? Is that so hard to believe? I did all kinds of things in my day. Still do when I can."

Paul held up his hands. "Whoa, now. I didn't mean no disrespect. I've been roofing for some years now, and I admire someone who knows first-hand how hard it is."

Paul fetched his ladder, put it in place, and climbed to the roof. He moved around carefully, stopping every so often to bend down for a closer look, and finished his inspection in twenty minutes or so.

"Some shingles need replacing, like you said, but all in all, she's in pretty fair shape," he said once he'd climbed down and done some figuring. "If I don't need more than a square, I should be able to match those shingles with ones in the truck. I can probably wrap it up this afternoon if that's agreeable."

"Same day service, eh? I like that. Let's you and me settle on a price, and then you can have a go at it."

Soon, Paul had fastened his tool belt, tied a red bandana around his head, and was slinging a bundle of shingles from his truck over one shoulder.

As he'd scaled the ladder, Martha admired the nimble and sure-footed way he moved around the steep roof.

When he'd finished with that bundle, he came down for another. He stopped when he found it waiting near the base of the ladder with a big glass of cold sweet tea resting on top. Paul shook his head, quickly polished off the tea, and picked up the bundle.

Another hour and he was finished. Martha came out on the porch. "All done?"

"Yes, ma'am. Didn't quite take two bundles. You want to take a look-see?"

Martha walked a few feet into the yard. With one hand shielding her eyes, she inspected the roof. "Looks real good. Can't hardly tell where you replaced them."

"Good. Glad you approve."

"I always approve of a job well done. Say, that sign on the truck says 'and More.' What does that mean, exactly?"

"Oh, that? It means different odd jobs. Like replacing a fence post or some rotted siding. Maybe fixing a gate that's sagging, or laying a slab for a shed. That sort of thing."

"You do all that?"

Paul's cheeks turned a little red. "Well, I'm not a professional or anything. More like a general handyman. But I do the best job I can and don't charge too steep."

Martha nodded. "Well, if you do as good as you done on the roof, I might just have a few more jobs for you."

"Yes, ma'am. That would be fine with me."

"That 'ma'am' of yours is starting to get on my nerves. Call me Martha. Say, Paul, I'm fixing to start supper. You're welcome to stay for a bite unless you need to get home to the missus."

"Nope," he said. "There's no missus. Not anymore." He stood silent for a few seconds, then said, "Supper sounds real good, Martha. Truth is, I could just about eat a horse."

Martha showed Paul where to wash up. "When you get back, take a seat there at the table while I'm fixing supper."

"Yes, ma'am." A glare from her made him hastily change it to Martha. When he returned, he pulled a chair from under the round oak table, sat down, and examined the lion claw feet it rested on. He gave the room a once-over and nodded his approval at the spotless fridge and stove. A cheerful wall calendar near the refrigerator showcased images of Norman Rockwell's monthly *Saturday Evening Post* covers. Even more arresting were the three magnificent black-and-white framed photos by Ansel Adams. He got up and went to inspect them more closely. Martha, while pulling out a cast iron skillet from a cabinet, looked over to see his reaction.

"Are those originals? Surely not."

Martha grinned. "Hard to believe, but they sure are. My late husband, Paul, took a photography workshop taught by Ansel in Yosemite Park back in the fifties. They got to be fast friends, and he sold them prints to James for a fraction of their worth."

"That's incredible. Your husband was a lucky man."

"James said them prints would make our retirement. But he never lived to see that." A tear trickled down her cheek, and she savagely brushed it away with the back of her hand. "Those was his treasure, and I keep them in the kitchen where I can see them every day. Sometimes I find that I lose track of time when I stare at them."

"Amazing."

"Yep. Say, is chops okay with you?"

"Just fine and dandy."

"Good, 'cause that's what I'm making." She used her big kitchen knife to indicate the calendar and photographs. "Them fellows sure knew their stuff."

Paul nodded. "Sure did. This is a nice place you've got here. Everything is spic and span."

"Ma brought me up knowing a thing or two about housekeeping, and I guess her lessons stuck with me."

Paul watched her as she worked. Middle age had not dulled her luster, and Paul thought what a fine figure of a woman she was. He imagined she'd had her share of attention, and he could almost see her as a teenager, the boys flocking. He also figured she hadn't given most of them the time of day.

At some point, she turned to look at him. She hesitated, then went ahead. "You said you no longer have a missus. Mind if I ask what happened? You don't have to talk about it if you don't want to."

Paul rubbed his chin. "Maggie was her name. We were married for five years. That woman lit up my life." At the word 'life,' his voice broke. "She died giving birth to our daughter, who followed her soon enough." He sat there, his eyes moist, looking lost, and forlorn.

Martha waited till she could speak. "I'm sorry, Paul. I shouldn't have asked. Didn't mean to cause you pain."

"It's all right. Sometimes it helps to talk about it."

Martha switched subjects. "Say, Paul, are diced potatoes and mustard greens, and cornbread, of course, good for you?"

"Absolutely, Martha. Sounds great."

"Alrighty, then. Supper should be ready soon. Now, how long you been in this line of work?"

"Going on thirty years. My daddy did carpentry work for a living. Many of the buildings in Hurlin bear his stamp. He taught me the trade, plus a lot of other things. I always liked working with my hands. Good, honest work that pays enough to get by. Ain't nothing like it for clearing my head and improving my outlook."

Martha smiled. "I sure do like the way you think. I was a farm girl, and it's stuck with me and served me well over the years. There's a lot to be said for doing work you enjoy."

Martha wiped her hands on a dishtowel she kept slung across her shoulder while she cooked. "Well, everything's ready. You mind getting the plates and glasses from that cabinet and setting the table?" She pointed. "The silverware is in that drawer right under."

"Be more than happy to, Martha."

During the meal, which Paul seemed to enjoy immensely, they talked about all manner of things. Upon the conclusion, he took the dishes to the sink while she put up the leftovers.

"Your cooking is first-rate, Martha. Don't know when I've had better. Sure is an improvement over what I fix myself."

"Glad to hear it. If you take on some of them other jobs of mine, you'll probably get another crack at my cooking."

"Maybe, in return, I can whittle down the price of the job a bit."

Martha smiled. "Alrighty, then. Now, do you want to wash or dry them dishes?"

A year later, when Tracy Scoggins, Martha's favorite niece, married Joe Conklin, the First Baptist Church of Hurlin was nearly overflowing.

It had rained that morning, and when the sun shone on the grass, it looked as if diamonds had been sprinkled among the green.

The day before, Paul and Martha had spent an hour in her rose garden, clipping all the pink and white roses that were ready. Now, the roses were wrapped in satin ribbon, and Tracy was examining them.

"Aunt Martha, this bouquet is the prettiest thing I've ever seen."

Martha touched Tracy's cheek. "Them roses can't hold a candle to you, Honey," she said.

When the "Wedding March" began to play, Martha was sitting on the front pew next to Paul, and he took her hand.

She was thinking of her first wedding day in another church, and how James had looked at her like she was a thing of wonder. But she was also thinking about the mystery of love, and how it can turn you inside out, even when you're as old as she is now.

She looked at the thin gold band Paul had given her just a month before, while the justice of the peace looked on. She still held up her hand and looked at it almost every day. It seemed like a miracle sitting there on her finger. She squeezed Paul's hand and stood to watch Tracy glide down the rose-strewn aisle.

# CHAPTER 27 — WHEN THINGS GO SOUTH

If Jeb Compton had an addiction, it came in the form of a small, wrinkled, split green "bean" imported from Columbia. Once roasted, ground, and brewed, it and its companions became a potent elixir that helped Jeb wake in the morning and sustained him through the coming day. In addition, the grounds provided further use as compost and fertilizer. His Annie had used them from time to time as a meat rub, and Jeb had even tried coffee grounds in the garden to ward off critters. This had varying success. The barn cats steered clear, as the smell apparently offended their sensibilities, but Homer, his large bluetick coonhound, evidently found their aroma enchanting.

"Homer, quit rolling around in the garden," Jeb called out. Homer uprighted himself and trotted over to Jeb, leaves, vines, and coffee grounds clinging to his coat. Jeb sighed and brushed off what he could. "I guess them grounds wasn't my best idea, but I would a thought your nose would take exception."

Jeb settled into his chair on the porch and thumbed through the *Hurlin Express*. "Hey, Homer, it say here that the old Bronson house is on the market. That's a strange critter, that house. I don't know who'd buy such a creation, but mayhap someone will. Someone, I would think, what didn't have much choice."

What makes a house a home? Bernice Craft wondered. She sat on the edge of the Queen Panel bed in the upstairs bedroom of the old house, which was called the Bronson House, and thought about it. She'd once posed that question to her best friend, Edna. Since Edna had gone through three husbands, Bernice questioned her wisdom on the subject. Nonetheless, she got an answer that sounded right to her. "When two people fall in love, get married, move into a house together, and have kids," Edna said, "then it becomes a home."

Bernice ran her hand across the chenille bedspread, feeling the tufts of soft cotton, and said out loud, "So, is that what went wrong with Earl and me — not filling all parts of the equation? I thought, in that Meatloaf song, he said three out of four ain't bad." She shook her head. "No, I guess it said two out of three. Same idea, though. Was he mistaken?" She addressed her question to Alphonse, the stuffed pink bunny with one black button eye. He sat on her pillow, staring at her with his impaired vision, but he didn't reply.

She reached over and grabbed the plush toy, cradled it in

her arms, then hugged it to her chest. I really should sew a button on him, she thought. Or, maybe, fashion a black pirate patch. That would give him a jaunty look, and the contrasting colors would really perk up his image.

Her mind drifted back in time. Earl had won that bunny for her at the fair soon after they were married, eight years ago. Squinting myopically, and throwing ball after ball as hard as he could with his spindly right arm, he spent all his pocket change trying with no success to knock over that bunny. Perhaps the carny took pity on him because Earl accomplished the feat with his last throw. He looked so proud when he presented it to her, and Alphonse had remained her companion and confidant ever since. Through good times and bad, Alphonse sat tall.

The bunny received his name, she thought, because she'd wanted one of the French variety. After all, hadn't they honeymooned in Paris? The fact that it was Paris, Arkansas, mattered not. Their limited budget didn't allow for much of a trip, much less one requiring a crossing of the Atlantic. Still, it didn't limit her imagination, and Alphonse came into being.

She placed the bunny in her lap and swatted her cheeks with her palms. Focus! she thought. She pulled her mind back into the proper channel: Earl and her, and what had gone wrong between them. That's what she needed to deal with. In the first two years of their marriage, they were madly in love. Money proved hard to come by in the early going, but Earl worked to become a successful accountant and build a clientele, and she'd begun substitute teaching at Hurlin's elementary school.

After a few lean years, they had saved enough to put a down payment on a house. They found the choices limited because of their sparse budget and settled for this one, the one the realtor called the Bronson House. It wasn't their first choice — or second, for that matter — but they could afford the payments, and it would serve.

In some ways, it appeared to be a typical Craftsman-style building with its covered front porch, supportive wooden columns set on bricked pillars, deep overhanging eaves, intricate woodwork, and steps leading up to the front porch. In other ways, not so much.

Someone — the architect, perhaps, in a drunken stupor — had added the two covered side patios. The typical multi-paned windows were nowhere to be found, and the second story had a railing and walkway across the width of the house. The roof slanted up at a proper forty-five-degree angle on each side, but the top was lopped off, and a row of curved tiles lay across it.

Bernice liked the quirky styling, and she'd adored the walkway. She could picture herself strolling back-and-forth on it, stopping now and then to search the bay for her husband's returning ship. The fact that the walkway actually overlooked a used car lot, and water only appeared when they washed the cars, did nothing to dampen her imagination.

She thought the symmetry of the house appealed to Earl's logical, orderly mind. He'd confirmed her hunch by adding two double-seated wooden benches, positioned an equal distance on either side of the front door, and dual porch lights properly spaced above the benches.

On a whim, she'd added a single mailbox. She thought this irritated him — this breaking of his sacred symmetry — but he just shook his head and left it there. Maybe he was putting up with his wife's eccentricities, or perhaps he acknowledged that adding a second mailbox would be a bit beyond the pale.

Upon completing their purchase, Earl had immediately

claimed the bottom floor for his office space, and Bernice voiced no objection. It made no sense to expect clients to climb another set of stairs, and she fancied the upstairs section more, anyway. After two more years, with Earl's business on the upswing, they decided the time to start a family had arrived.

Despite their best efforts, Bernice did not conceive. Medical visits proved futile, and they gave up hope. Earl threw himself into his work, and Bernice languished for a time trying to stave off bouts of depression. She found wine helpful in getting through those. Earl grew more distant. Looking back, she thought, perhaps it worked out for the best. If children were necessary to save a marriage, maybe it lacked strength to begin with.

She shook her head and smiled at Alphonse. "Well, bunny, at least Earl and I had fun trying for kids, and I do apologize for all those times you ended up on the floor." Bernice didn't believe that a button could wink, but she swore she saw Alphonse toss her one. "Alphonse," she said, frowning, "I miss those days." She placed him back on his pillow and went downstairs.

Squaring her shoulders, she pushed open the door to Earl's office. When he looked up from his figures, his eyebrows raised.

"Bernice, you surprised me. You don't come in here much. What can I do for you?"

"Earl," she said, "I — no, we need to talk."

Two hours later, as Bernice finished loading the brown vinyl suitcase, she looked over at Alphonse. "Well, bunny, I tried. I really did. But I guess Earl and I have grown too far apart to bring back together. Or, maybe we're just too different. At any rate —" The words trickled off, and she stood there. No, she thought, I'm not going to cry. There will

186

be time enough for that later. "At any rate, we're calling it quits. We're going to put the house up for sale and try to get on with our lives. I hate to do this, but you're going to have to stay here. There would be too much hurt in seeing you wherever I end up. Too many memories you would dredge up. And who knows, maybe you can bring some joy to somebody else like you did to me."

Bernice gave Alphonse a last hug and settled him back on the pillow. Squaring her shoulders, she picked up the suitcase, walked down the stairs, and went out the front door. When she reached the sidewalk, she turned around and looked at the house. "I'll miss you, too, old house. Be safe." She turned and walked away to an uncertain future.

## CHAPTER 28 — FILLING NEEDS

The package showed up on Jeb's front porch one crisp October morning, accompanied by Homer's excited barking. It stood about four feet high and weighed around seventy pounds. It came wrapped in a green sweater, red-and-black plaid skirt, knee-high striped socks, and brown shoes with red laces. It had curly red hair, green eyes, a snub nose, and freckles. The package also came with an unhappy expression and a large suitcase. Emily, Jeb's ten-year-old niece, had arrived.

The Department of Human Services caseworker's words were not unkind, but they were matter of fact. "Mr. Compton, I know the death of your sister in that terrible accident has you deeply upset, but think of the child. You are her only surviving relative we can find."

Jeb sat in the office chair at the DHS, his elbow on the armrest and his hand over his bowed head. When he looked up, he said, "Annie and I never had no kids, and I don't know nothing about raising them. I live alone. Just me and my hound. Used to have me a goat, too, but that didn't work out. Anyway, I spend a chunk of each day farming, and I be set in my ways. That be no fit place for a little girl to come into. Ain't fair to her."

The caseworker's voice chilled. "Fair? Nothing about this is fair. It's not fair that she lost her mother. It's not fair that she has no siblings to share her grief and talk to. It's not fair that her only relative we can find doesn't seem to want her."

Jeb's eyes flashed. "Now you just hold on there, Missy. I didn't say I didn't want her. I'm just afraid I can't be giving her what she needs."

"If that's the case, then the only alternative is for her to become a ward of the state."

"What do that mean?"

"Well, she'll be designated a foster child and be placed with people who agree to act as her guardians. The state will cover her expenses in exchange for them agreeing to supply her with a home. In some cases, children remain wards of the state till they become eighteen."

Jeb turned that over in his head. "Those foster home people, do they be good folk?"

The caseworker hesitated. She studied Jeb and reached a decision. "I probably shouldn't say this because it's not government policy, but I've taken a shine to that little girl. So, yes. Many of them are, and they do have to become state-certified to foster children."

"I is sensing a 'but' here."

"But there are far too many cases of child abuse, physical neglect, chronic medical problems, and emotional deprivation."

Jeb stared at the floor and let that soak in.

Annie's voice, from times past, entered his thoughts unbidden. "Jeb, you pull some bone-headed stunts sometimes, but you are a good man who does the right thing — most times, anyway. That's why I love you. Just don't never forget that family is everything."

He looked at the caseworker. "Okay, then. I'll do the best I can for Emily, and Lord help us both. Go ahead and get them guardianship papers ready, and I'll sign."

Jeb picked up the suitcase and held the door open for Emily. "Go ahead on in, young lady." He pointed with his free hand. "That hall takes you to the living room. Grab you a seat and get comfortable while I put this here case in your room."

He returned to find Emily standing by the window, staring out. "Ain't much to see, but I sometime watch for them bobwhite quail," Jeb said. "I like to listen to their calls and watch 'em scurry about. They help keep them ticks down, too." Emily did not reply, so Jeb tried another tack. "Say, you hungry? I can rustle up something. Eggs and bacon, maybe? Or biscuits and gravy?"

Emily continued to look out the window. "I'm not hungry."

Jeb tried again. "Well, then, what would you like to do? I don't have to mess with them soybeans today, so I be free and clear. Maybe you and me and my old hound Homer can go for a ride." Silence filled the room. Jeb blew out a breath.

"Emily, we going to be living together. We need to talk to each other and figure out how things are going to be, don't you think?"

Emily turned and looked at Jeb. "You talk funny."

Jeb blinked. "I do?"

"Yes. You don't talk like people in Columbus, Ohio. They use proper English."

If Jeb was offended, he didn't let on. "Well, it's true that I ain't got a lot of book learning. Didn't get too far up in school 'cause I had to help my folks with the crops. Is how I talk such a bad thing?"

"Of course it is. My mom says —"

Emily went silent. A tear ran down her cheek. She wiped it away with the sleeve of her sweater and stood trembling with fists clenched at her sides.

Jeb's eyes widened in alarm. "Whoa now, Emily. It's gonna be okay. We'll work things out. And it's okay to talk about your ma." Jeb touched the center of his chest. "Even though she done departed this world, she's still right here."

Emily yelled loud enough to set Homer howling. She stamped her foot. "It's not okay! Nothing is okay. Not me. Not you. Not this place. Nothing is okay." She ran past Jeb, down the hall, and out the door. The screen door slammed shut behind her.

Jeb stood rooted to the floor. What in tarnation just happened? he wondered. He headed for the front door, but as soon as he touched the frame of the screen door, he worried that going after Emily would be the wrong thing to do. Jeb looked heavenward and asked his Annie for a thimbleful of advice, but his departed wife stayed silent.

Jeb stuck his head out and spotted Emily. She was kneeling on the ground near the end of the porch with her arms locked tight around Homer's neck and her head buried in his coarse fur. Her shoulders heaved as she cried. Homer stood with his legs locked and his big head resting gently on Emily's shoulder. He looked over at Jeb as if to say, "It's okay. I got a handle on this."

After a few minutes, when Emily's sobs subsided, Jeb walked over to them and stood quietly by. Emily finally looked up at Jeb through red-rimmed eyes and sniffed. "Your dog smells funny."

Jeb laughed, knelt down beside them, and rubbed the top of Homer's head. "That he do. Say, why don't we go sit on the porch. I got some lemonade in the refrigerator if you is interested."

Emily sat in one of the white oak chairs, and Jeb got the drinks. He handed her one. "Hope I didn't make it too sweet for you."

She took a small sip, followed by a larger one. "It's good."

"Glad you like it. My Annie used to say she didn't need to ring no dinner bell. She could just set a bowl of sugar on an open window ledge, and I'd come a running."

"Who's Annie?"

In a choked voice, Jeb said, "I guess your ma didn't tell you much about us. After your dad disappeared, and you and your ma moved away, we kind of lost touch with each other. Annie, she were my wife. She died aways back from the cancer. Not a day goes by when I don't think of her."

Emily sat quietly, staring at her glass. "So you've lost someone, too."

Jeb sniffed and wiped at his eyes. "I did. And Emily, I knowed the hurt and pain that settles in your bones. Sometimes, it seems more than one can bear. And it do get lonely. That's why I think we can make this work, Emily. Why we owe it to ourselves to try. We both been through something awful, but maybe we can pull together to make things better."

Emily hesitated. Homer, who'd been sitting at Jeb's feet, got up, padded over, and laid his head in Emily's lap. "That be Homer's way of saying he's willing to do his part. What do you say?"

Emily said in a small voice, "I think I'd like that."

## CHAPTER 29 — PRECOCIOUS

Emily's small, compact body, topped by red Shirley Temple curls, hurtled through Jeb Compton's front door. The screen door was flung rudely open and pitched back and forth in Emily's wake. "Uncle Jeb! Homer's got his head caught!"

Jeb, barefoot with shirt halfway buttoned, barged out the front door and onto his porch. He stopped abruptly and stared at the spectacle in front of him. "Again? Dang it, Homer. How in the name of all that's holy did you get your head stuck in that minnow bucket? Hold on, and I'll try to get it off."

Jeb gripped the sides of the bucket, gritted his teeth, and yanked. The bucket stayed firmly in place. A heavy round of tugging, grunting, and yelping commenced, and Homer's large head finally popped free. The hound plopped back on his butt, and Jeb staggered back a few steps. "I swear, Homer."

He stopped short. Homer stood with head bowed, tail tucked, and a woebegone look on his face. Jeb reached down and ruffled the furry head. "It's okay, boy. I done my share of stupid in my day, so I needn't be upset with you."

With Homer a free hound once more, Jeb returned to finish dressing, then went to the kitchen to make breakfast. Halfway through her plate of scrambled eggs, bacon, and toast, Emily paused. "Homer isn't very smart."

Jeb considered. "I reckon not. He and me kind of have that in common, I 'spect."

Emily sniffed dismissively and stuck her snub nose in the air. "If you say so, but at least you never got your head stuck in a bucket." Jeb choked a bit and turned it into a cough to cover up. Best not mention those times I got sloshed with my coon hunting buddies, he thought. A head stuck in a bucket were the least of the stunts we pulled.

Emily continued, "Dogs can be quite stupid."

Jeb felt his ears start to turn red. "Now, that's about enough, Missy. There be a big difference twixt being stupid and doing something stupid now and again. That second part is where Homer fits, and I 'spect a lot of us humans, too."

Emily lowered her head, so Jeb tried a more conciliatory approach. "You know, Emily, a fella named Emerson once said, 'Character is higher than intellect. A great soul will be strong to live as well as think.' Now, old Homer, he got himself a heap of character and a real fine soul. And he do more living than most folk I know."

"Well, I still think —"

Jeb cut her off. "Emily, we be done talking right now. Finish your breakfast so I can wash up them dishes."

Tears welled in Emily's eyes. She jumped up from her

chair, ran down the hall, pulled open the front door, and escaped outside.

Jeb rubbed his temples. His thoughts turned to his sweet Annie, and he spoke aloud to her as he often did since her death. "Well, Annie, I guess I didn't handle that none too good. Wish you was here to dispense some wisdom."

Jeb listened, hoping his wife would send him a sign. When she didn't, he said, "Okay, Annie, I reckon I'd best give Emily a minute before I go try to mend some fences."

When Jeb looked out his front door, he saw Emily sitting on the porch. Her short legs dangled off the edge, and she had her right arm draped over Homer, who appeared to be listening intently as Emily talked.

"I'm sorry, Homer," Emily said. "I didn't mean to insult you like that. I'm sure you're smart enough, most of the time, and you —" She scrunched up her face in concentration. "You have a heap of character and a real fine soul. I hope you'll forgive me."

Homer gave Emily a big, sloppy lick, barked, and bounded off the porch, likely in search of a rabbit to chase. Emily looked up to see Jeb smiling at her.

"That were a right nice apology, Emily. I know Homer appreciated it."

If Emily was embarrassed, she didn't show it. "Well, I might have been a little hard on him. I should have been more sympathetic. Are you still mad at me?"

"No. I guess you just hit a sore spot. You see, Emily, my Annie give Homer to me our last Christmas together. He's been by my side ever since, and he helped me over some real rough patches. It were upsetting to hear you say them things about him, but you apologized, and Homer didn't take no offense, so let's you and me forget all about it."

"That Emerson fellow you talked about. Do you have

something he wrote I can look at?"

"Might you be wanting something more fitted to your age, though?"

"No. Most of the books the girls in my grade read are boring."

"Well, I think I got a book of his essays laying around here somewheres. It don't be the easiest reading, but it sure do give you a lot to ponder. I'll see if I can find it after I clean up."

"Okay," she said. "If you'll wash and rinse the dishes, I'll dry and put them up."

"That be good of you, Emily, but you don't have to do that."

Emily drew herself up to her full height. "Yes, I do. I need to pull my weight around here."

After the dishes were finished, Jeb went out to tend his soybeans. He left Emily curled up on the sofa with the Emerson essays and smiled at the furious look of concentration on her face. He returned around noon to fix lunch and check on her. Emily sat in the same place he'd left her. Shaking his head, he headed to the kitchen to set the table.

"Emily! Come here a minute."

She came into the kitchen. "Yes, Uncle Jeb?"

"What in tarnation have you done to the cabinets? Everything's all switched around on me."

Emily smiled. "Oh, I decided to arrange things more —" She paused while hunting for the word. "Efficiently. It makes a lot more sense now."

Jeb frowned. "Not to me, it don't. You should have asked before you took this on yourself."

Emily's smile disappeared. "I'm sorry. I thought it would please you."

Jeb reined in his annoyance. "Well, I 'spose I'll get used to it. I didn't mean to snap at you. Just caught me by surprise is all." He smiled at her. "Emily, it be good of you to want to help out and all, but do you think you might check with me first next time?"

"Yes, Uncle Jeb."

Jeb changed the subject. "How you coming with old Emerson?"

Emily's eyes brightened. "Oh, he's really something. He's kind of hard to read, like you said, but he's got some wonderful thoughts. I've got a whole bunch of questions."

"Do you, now? Well, I tell you what. After I work a couple more hours on them beans, why don't we set a spell on the porch and talk on it? We can make up some lemonade. I find lemonade and Emerson go real good together. What say?"

"That sounds wonderful. I'll write down my questions while you're gone."

"Okay, then. Now, would you mind setting the table while I rustle us up some lunch?"

That evening, they sat on the porch with lemonade in hand. Emily plunged right in. "What does it mean when he says, 'A foolish consistency is the hobgoblin of little minds.'?"

Jeb considered. "Well, to me, it means it be foolish to do the same thing time and again for no better reason than that's the way it's always been done."

Emily grinned. "You mean like the way you stored your dishes?"

Jeb shot her a long look but didn't take the bait. "I think it's more like figuring out the right or wrong of something for yourself and not just going along to get along."

Annie nodded. "That makes sense. Now, what does he mean —"

After an hour of this, Jeb felt like he'd gone three rounds

with a prizefighter. He desperately looked around for someone to throw in the towel. Homer came bounding up on the porch and barked. Bless you, dog, he thought. "Well, Emily, we is going to have to leave off now."

Emily frowned. "Do we have to?"

"Yes, ma'am, we do. Homer be wanting his supper, and I'm a mite hungry my own self."

Emily sighed. "Okay, but can we do this again?"

Jeb smiled. "Surely can. And Emily, maybe tomorrow we can run into town and see about getting you a library card."

Emily jumped up, hugged Jeb's book to her chest, spun in a circle, and shot off to the kitchen. Jeb stood stiffly, grimaced as he stretched, paused to pat Homer, then followed at a considerably slower pace.

# Chapter 30 — Conference Call

The phone rang four times before a barefoot Jeb Compton entered the kitchen. In his rush to answer, he stubbed his toe on the kitchen table leg, and the phone rang once more as he hopped around and cussed. After, Jeb grabbed the receiver, his "Hello" sounding less than inviting.

A female voice asked, "Is this Jeb Compton?"

"This be him."

"This is Connie Elmore, Emily's teacher. I'm sorry to be calling so early, but I hoped to catch you before you left for work. Do you have a moment?"

Jeb's toe throbbed. "What's this about?"

"I'm afraid Emily's having a few problems at school, and I'd like to schedule a conference after school so we could talk about them."

Jeb sucked in his breath. "She in trouble?"

"No, it's not like that. It's more of an adjustment problem. Do you think you could come by today? Say around four o'clock?"

Jeb sighed. "I'll be there. Where should I come to?"

"The fifth-grade classroom is on the first floor. You will need to check in at the office first. It's across from the main doors. They will direct you."

"Okay, then."

"Thank you, Mr. —" the teacher said, but Jeb had already hung up.

That afternoon, Jeb tied Homer to the big sycamore near the porch. "Sorry, old boy. I know you be wanting to run free and raise a ruckus, but the traffic's bad this time of day, and I don't want you getting hurt. I hope not to be gone too long."

The big bluetick gave Jeb a suffering look then lay down for a nap. Jeb fired up his old Ford truck and headed for the elementary school. He pulled into the parking lot and saw the row of ungainly buses lined up to transport the students. He waited till the bell rang and watched the building disgorge its contents as students poured out the front door. When he saw Emily, he hollered her name and waved her over. Emily sped over and hopped in the truck. "Hi, Uncle Jeb. What are you doing here?"

"Got a call from your teacher. She's wanting a conference in a bit, and I don't want you coming home to an empty house. Just wait in the truck while I'm in there."

Emily sat quietly, her hands in her lap. "Am I in trouble?"

"I don't get that feeling, so don't you worry your head about it. I'll know more soon. You stay in the truck now."

A few minutes later, Jeb paused in the doorway to survey Emily's classroom. Four rows of brown oak desks with a straight-backed oak chair fitted under each filled most of the space. A shelf under each desk held books and supplies. The vile mustard-colored walls were broken up; on one side, there were three shaded windows. On the other, there were several cork bulletin boards filled with battered posters, students' work, and printed materials.

Across the front wall were three dark green chalkboards. Yellow chalk and erasers filled the trays beneath. A large, circular clock above the middle chalkboard ticked away the minutes. The teacher's desk and chair sat in front of the chalkboards. Only by its larger size and placement could the desk be distinguished from all the others. This ain't much different from my school days, Jeb thought. More's the pity.

"Mr. Compton?"

Jeb flinched but checked himself from jumping or wheeling around to face the voice. He turned and said, "I'm him."

A pleasant-looking woman smiled at him. Jeb judged her to be in her mid-to-late forties, a few years younger than his own age, and she stood about four inches shy of his six-foot height. Her hair shone a golden brown that reminded him of autumn wheat. Pale blue eyes, with mild crow's feet at the corners, framed a straight nose above a mouth with generous lips. Jeb admired the view, then immediately felt guilty for doing so.

"Hello, Mr. Compton. I'm Connie Elmore. It's nice to meet you. Would you please come in and take a seat?"

Jeb pulled out a chair and sat awkwardly on a seat made for smaller frames, while the teacher sat behind her desk. Seeing his struggles, she chuckled. "I'm sorry, Mr. Compton. That was rude. Won't you please use my chair?"

Jeb snorted. "That be all right. I'll make do. Now, what's this about Emily?"

Mrs. Elmore's face grew serious. "Let me start by saying that I adore Emily. She is smart, friendly, sensitive, full of life, and interested in everything."

Jeb smiled. "She's that, all right."

"That said, she can also be stubborn, willful, opinionated, and exhausting to the extreme."

If Mrs. Elmore had expected a protest from Jeb, she didn't get one. Jeb gave a rueful smile. "Seems you got her pegged all around."

"You've noticed this too?"

"A man would have to be deaf and blind not to."

"Has she always been like this?"

"I 'spect so, but it's hard to say. Emily only come to me this last month."

Mrs. Elmore looked confused. "I'm not sure what you mean."

Jeb explained the situation by which Emily had become his responsibility.

"I'm so sorry. I didn't know."

He scratched his ear and smiled. "It's all right. We're getting adjusted to each other. Kind of. It be a work in progress."

"I imagine so. Well, her problems at school aren't due to her coming in after semester. They mostly stem from her advanced intellect."

"Say what, now?"

"Well, she gets easily bored with the lessons. When we are discussing literature, for example, she says it's not complex enough. Then, of all things, she throws out a quote from Emerson. Emerson! Nobody in class knows who she's talking about. Where did she even hear about him?"

Jeb mumbled his answer.

"I'm sorry. Did you say something?"

Jeb cleared his throat. "I guess maybe I'm responsible for that."

Mrs. Elmore frowned. "You?"

That hit Jeb wrong, and he flared up. "Yes, me. You think an ignorant soybean farmer can't know nothing about Emerson?"

A spark of fear shown in Connie's eyes. Seeing this, Jeb immediately regretted his outburst.

"Calm down, Mr. Compton. I didn't know you were a soybean farmer, and I certainly don't think you're ignorant. It just surprised me that anybody knows anything about Emerson."

Jeb took a breath. "I'm sorry. I didn't get too far in school, and I guess I be touchy about that. But I do love to read, and I'm interested in history and men what be known for they big thoughts. Emerson fitted right in there."

Emily's teacher smiled. "Apology accepted, and I think you should be proud for not letting circumstances hold you back."

"Nice of you to say so. What else is Emily pulling?"

"Well, I noticed when she gets deeply involved in something that's a challenge to her, she doesn't want to put it aside. That's a problem when I have to move on to another subject."

Jeb nodded. "I seen that side of her. I also seen that she be having her own way of doing things."

"Yes, and while I'm not one to push the idea that there's only one way to do something, I teach that way because my tried and true method will always get you the answer. Some of Emily's approaches take a little time getting there if they arrive at all."

Jeb nodded again. "How do she get along with them other kids?"

"She's friendly and outgoing, so pretty well, usually. There was this one incident the other day, though."

Jeb raised his eyebrows. "Incident?"

"It happened on the playground. Some of the boys were tormenting a toad, and she got upset. She got even more upset after confronting them because they wouldn't stop. I kept her from assaulting them and rescued the toad. I tried to help her understand that sometimes, even when you're right, people aren't going to go along with you."

Jeb chuckled. "I'm proud of her for that, but I see why you be needing to prevent bloodshed."

"Anyway, I wanted to make you aware of some things with Emily, but it seems you pretty much already are."

"Some, but I'll keep me a watchful eye out in the days to come."

"I appreciate that. If we both keep working with her, we may be able to make her path a little easier. For her and for the rest of us."

A knock sounded, and Emily poked her head in the door. Jeb threw her a stern look. "I thought I told you to wait in the truck."

"I know. I'm sorry, but you were taking so long that I thought I'd better check on you. And I'm getting kind of hungry." Mrs. Elmore and Jeb both laughed.

"Well, I guess we can wrap this up for now. Thank you for coming by, Mr. Compton, especially on short notice."

"That's fine, Mrs. Elmore," Jeb said.

She held out her hand to shake his.

"Knowing Emily," Jeb said, "it might not be the last time."

"Uncle Jeb!"

Jeb grinned. "Come on, Emily. Let's get you home and see if I'm able to keep you from starving. I expect Homer will be wanting his supper, too."

On the drive home, Emily looked over at Jeb. "So, am I in trouble?"

"We can have that conversation after dinner, young lady, but the short answer be no."

Emily blew out a breath. "What did you think of Miss Elmore?"

"She's a real nice lady. Wait, don't you mean Mrs. Elmore?"

"Nope. I didn't notice a ring on her finger, so I did some checking. I couldn't get all the details, but I found out that she's divorced. That means she was married but isn't anymore, right?"

"That's what it means, but why the snooping?"

"Oh, no reason. Don't you think she's pretty? I mean, for an older lady."

Jeb swallowed. "I think I be needing to concentrate on my driving right now. Let's hold off on the talking till later."

Emily smiled. "Whatever you say, Uncle Jeb."

## CHAPTER 31 — TURNING POINT

Jeb Compton wiped Emily's face with a cool, damp washcloth. She stirred but did not open her eyes. Her forehead still felt a bit warm to his touch, and her cheeks were faintly flushed, but she seemed to be breathing easier. He set the cloth in the washbasin and dried his hands. Gazing down at her sleeping face, he reached out his hand and smoothed her hair with a light touch. Heavens to Betsy, he sure did love that little girl.

Next, he headed to the phone. After making arrangements through the school office to pick up Emily's assignments from her teacher at four o'clock the next day, he hung up and began supper.

Miss Connie Elmore looked up as Jeb rapped on the door jamb of her classroom. "Hello, Mr. Compton; nice to see you again. Please have a seat. I hope Emily is feeling better."

Jeb took the same under-sized chair he'd used before. "That flu sure enough took her down a peg, but yes, ma'am, she's some better. Doc Wilkens say she probably be able to come back in a day or two."

Miss Elmore handed Jeb a manila folder bulging with papers. "That's good news. Here are the assignments Emily's missed. It won't take her long to catch up."

"How she be doing these days?"

Miss Elmore smiled. "Really well. She's managed to tone down some of her opinions while not losing her enthusiasm. Here, let me give you something else to take with you."

While she rummaged around in her desk drawer, Jeb admired the teacher's hair. It was such a nice color, and it looked so soft and shiny. Before Jeb could stop himself, he wondered what it would feel like to hold a lock of it between his calloused fingers. The unbidden thought did two things: it made him blush, and it made him feel as if he were betraying his sweet Annie.

When he was finally able to look at Miss Elmore, she was handing him one of Emily's finished assignments. He scanned the top page, and his eyes were drawn to the red, circled A in the top right-hand corner. "Wonderful!" was written below the grade in an elegant script.

Miss Elmore pointed at the A. "Emily said this was her second try, that her first got eaten by your dog. What do you make of that?"

Jeb covered his mouth. Muffled noises escaped, and Miss Elmore could most certainly see his shoulders shaking. She cocked an eyebrow. Jeb gave it up then and let his laugh roll free. He wiped at his eyes with the back of his hand and tried to regain his composure. "I think that's real possible. Emily do her school work at the kitchen table, usually in the company of a peanut butter sandwich. Now my dog, Homer, he do love peanut butter. If she happened to get some smeared on her paper, and she left it where he could get at it, that would draw him like a magnet draws nails."

Miss Elmore nodded. "I see. Well, it's a marvelous essay. I told the class to write about a favorite poem, and she picked one by Edna St. Vincent Millay. Millay is not even in our literature text, and her poetry is not covered till ninth grade."

Jeb scratched his head. "Well, Emily's done gone through all my books with a fine-tooth comb. She might a come across one of Millay's in there, and we maybe discussed it a little bit."

Miss Elmore tilted her head and looked at Jeb for a few seconds before speaking. "I thought as much. First, you introduced her to Emerson, and now Millay. You certainly are an interesting man, Mr. Compton."

Jeb squirmed in his chair, and his eyes refused to meet hers. "Nah, I'm just an old soybean farmer who likes to read some."

"Well, I think it's wonderful. Emily's mind is like a sponge: it soaks up everything she's curious about. You're helping her to develop that mind."

Jeb still couldn't meet her eyes. "That's right nice of you to say. That little girl has done gone through a heap of trouble, and I want to do what I can for her."

"Well, I admire that, and I think you're doing a fine job."

Jeb stood, gathered Emily's materials, looked at Miss Elmore, and cleared his throat. "I should be getting to the house. It will soon be feeding time for my two, and I best be ready."

At the classroom door, he looked back. "For what it be

worth, I think you're good for Emily, too. She talks about you a bunch." It was Miss Elmore's turn to blush.

When Jeb got home, he checked on Emily and found her sitting up in her bed. Homer lay beside her and looked guilty when Jeb's eyes fixed on him. "Homer, you varmint, what you doing there? I didn't know you was even in the house. Were you hiding out till I left?"

Homer whined, and Emily grinned. "He came creeping in as soon as you left. Don't be mad at him, Uncle Jeb. He just wanted to check up on me."

Jeb shook his head. "Well, what's done is done. How you feeling?"

Emily's reply came in a rapid-fire burst. "I'm much better. I can't wait to get back to school. Did you get the assignments I missed?"

Jeb laughed. "Whoa. Slow it down, Missy. Yes, I got your assignments."

Emily's eyes brightened. "Good. Can I get started on them right now, please?"

"Are you sure you be a real human child?"

Emily grinned. "About half, I think. So can I?"

"Let's get some food in you two first, and then we'll see."

Emily pretended to pout but couldn't sustain it. Then, she asked, "Did you see Miss Elmore?"

Jeb blinked. "Course I did. Them papers of yours didn't just show up in my truck."

"Did she look as pretty as ever?"

Jeb frowned. "She be a nice-looking woman, yes. What are you getting at?"

"Oh, nothing."

"Well, then, I'll be getting supper on."

"Uncle Jeb?"

"What?"

Emily looked down at Homer, and Jeb could swear the hound nodded. She looked back up at Jeb. "Do you think you might —" Emily stalled for a second. "Do you think you might, well, maybe ask her to go with us sometime. You know, like to maybe a movie or something?"

"What are earth is you thinking?"

"Well, when I last saw you two together, you were talking, and it looked like you were both enjoying yourselves."

Jeb snorted. "That were just a conference. About you, if you recollect."

"I know, but still —"

Jeb opened his mouth, but Emily jumped back in. "I know you must get lonely with no one but Homer and me around. I think Miss Elmore gets lonely too. She looks sad sometimes, though she tries not to show it."

Jeb held up his hand, palm outward, and scowled. "That's enough of this. It's something that don't concern you. Now, I got supper to tend to." He turned and left the room.

Later that night, after a decidedly subdued meal, Emily took her folder and went to her room. Jeb retired to the porch, where he sat in his favorite chair. Homer followed and lay nearby gazing up at him as if the old boy was accusing him of something. Jeb tried looking elsewhere, but he could still feel the hound's eyes boring into him.

"I know, all right? I didn't handle that none too good. Emily just caught me unawares. You know, Homer, my Annie and me had thirty good years together, and I loved that woman something fierce. It just don't seem right to be casting eyes on another woman. It seem disloyal to Annie's memory and makes me feel guilty. And who knows how that teacher lady feels about things? She were married, but that went south. Maybe she's burnt out on men after that. And even if she ain't, what would a pretty, educated lady like her see in an old coot like me?"

Homer stood up, padded over, and lay his big head on Jeb's knee. Jeb stroked the coarse fur and sighed. "It's a real puzzle now, ain't it?"

"Uncle Jeb?"

Jeb jumped. "Emily. You give me a start, young lady. What you doing out here?"

Barefoot and in her nightdress, Emily stood with eyes downcast. "I came to tell you I was sorry for making you upset, and I heard you out here talking to Homer."

Jeb closed his eyes for a moment. "So, you heard that, huh?"

She looked up, then dropped her gaze again. "Well, not all of it. But most of it, I guess."

Jeb blew out a breath he hadn't known he was holding. "I see."

Emily looked miserable. "I'm sorry."

Jeb walked over to Emily and rested a hand on her head. "It's okay, Emily. You didn't do nothing wrong."

Emily gave a sob and threw her arms around Jeb, and Jeb hugged her. "Tell you what. Tomorrow I'll head over to the cemetery, and Annie and me will have a little talk. See if we can sort things out. You go on to bed, and I'll tell you how things stand when I know something. That be okay?"

Emily wiped her eyes. "You talked to Homer about Annie and how you miss her. I feel the same about my mom. Could you tell me a little about the times you and my mom spent together?"

Jeb felt his heart crack. "Sure thing, Emily. Let's sit down. Put your feet up on Homer. He won't mind none." When they were seated, he resumed.

"We had rough times back then in California. Weren't never enough to eat, and we didn't have no decent clothes.

We had to work the fields with Ma to get by. In spite of that, Ellie never gave up, and things got better when we was back in Oklahoma. I truly loved your ma. She were smart as a whip, and we was thick as thieves when we was kids. Your ma could throw a baseball like a boy, and bale hay like one too. But when she got to be, let's see, twelve or so, she give it all up and started wearing hair ribbons and such."

Emily listened intently. "She thought well of you, too, Uncle Jeb. Thank you for telling me."

"It be fine, Emily, and we can do it again, but right now, you best get off to bed. Don't want you getting knocked down a peg when you still be on the mend."

Emily stood up and bent down to hug Jeb. "Goodnight, Uncle Jeb. I love you."

Jeb choked up, but returned the hug. "Goodnight, Emily. I love you, too."

# CHAPTER 32 — THE GIFT

Christmas approached, and the city of Hurlin readied itself. Workers strung lights on the courthouse and erected the manger scene. In the square, the twenty-foot fir tree — hauled in, placed and braced — stood proudly in its coat of ribbons, ornaments, and lights. Merchants' decorated windows were accented with signs proclaiming big sales events. Townsfolk swelled the sidewalks in greater numbers, and they moved with buoyant steps.

Jeb sat in his chair on his porch with Homer sprawled out on the worn oak planks. Sharing the companionable silence of a newly dawned day, save for a few bird calls, had become a custom with these two. But today, Jeb wanted to talk.

"Homer, Christmas be coming, and I'm needing to come up with the right present for Emily. It's our first Christmas with my niece after all. You got any ideas?"

The big hound yawned, stretched, and ambled over to the small wooden stool Emily had claimed for her own soon after she'd arrived at Jeb's. He nosed the book she had left on the seat. Jeb's eyes widened. "Homer, did you just understand what I were saying? That thought's a mite unsettling."

Homer nosed the book again and licked the cover. Jeb retrieved the book, took a look, and then a sniff. He laughed. "I might a knowed. It's got peanut butter smeared on the cover. Still, you give me an idea here. Emily do love to read, but the books is all my old ones or from the library. She might just like some of her very own. But which ones? I could ask her, but that there would ruin the surprise."

Homer stared at Jeb a moment, then barked. He nudged the paper and pencil Emily had used to take notes. "Now don't mess with them, Homer. They for her school work."

The words triggered an epiphany. Jeb realized Emily's teacher, Miss Elmore, would know just what books to get. If he picked Emily up from school, he could ask her in person.

The thought of seeing the teacher stirred a pot of mixed emotions, with equal measures of excitement, anticipation, unease, and guilt. Despite a trip to the cemetery to visit his Annie, he still hadn't resolved his feelings about Miss Elmore. Well, Jeb thought, I do still need to find out about them books.

After intercepting Emily as she left the school, and asking her to wait in the truck, Jeb went to Miss Elmore's room and knocked on the door.

"Come in," Miss Elmore said as she was erasing the chalkboard. She had a smudge of chalk on her cheek, and Jeb found that charming.

She smiled. "Mr. Compton. This is a surprise. We weren't scheduled for a conference, were we?"

"No, ma'am, but I were wondering if you could spare a few minutes."

"Of course. What can I do for you?"

Jeb took his usual seat, and Miss Elmore sat behind her desk. Jeb's eyes kept wandering to that chalk smudge until she quirked an eyebrow. His ears reddened. "I'm sorry. You just be wearing a bit of chalk dust on your cheek."

Miss Elmore wiped her cheek with a tissue. "I can't seem to stay clear of the stuff. One day I went to the office for something. I turned to leave, and I'd left a trail of footprints on the carpet."

"Well, I think you got it."

"So, what's on your mind?"

Jeb explained his predicament and asked for suggestions. Miss Elmore grabbed a pen and paper and looked up with sparkling eyes. "Oh, yes, I can definitely recommend some great books. I'll write them down as I think of them. Some are advanced, but it's Emily we're talking about. Let's see. For fantasy, there's *A Wrinkle in Time* and *The Hobbit*. For dystopian, there's *Animal Farm* and *Fahrenheit 451*."

She paused in thought, tapping the pen against her chin. "Oh! Let's add *The Old Man and the Sea*, and of course, *To Kill a Mockingbird*. And *Jonathan Livingston Seagull*. Hmm."

Jeb noted the small crease in her brow as she pondered, and the triumph on her face when she thought of another book. This was a woman, he thought, who set to her task and took no quarter.

When Miss Elmore finally ran down, she seemed deflated but happy. She folded the paper, walked over to Jeb, and handed it to him. "Emily can't go wrong with any of these. I can't wait to hear her go on about them."

Jeb carefully raised himself from the undersized student chair and tried to avoid the desire to stretch out his aching back. "Thank you kindly. I'm sure these here will be a hit with her."

"You're very welcome. I wish all solutions could be achieved this easily."

Jeb looked up from the list. "Something bothering you?"

"Oh, this and that, little things, really. But there is one bigger concern, and I'm not sure what to do about it."

Jeb looked at her and waited.

Miss Elmore sighed. "I've got several students whose parents are not at all well off. We have a national school lunch program that provides those students breakfast and lunch, but they need so much more: school supplies, warm jackets, decent shoes, and clothes. I don't have the funds to supply them, and it really bothers me." She grimaced. "But here I am going on. I'm sorry. You're such an easy man to talk to."

Jeb's throat had gone tight, and he swallowed before he spoke. "That's all right. I don't mind none. I hope your problem somehow works out."

"Perhaps it will."

Jeb said his goodbyes and went to his truck, deep in thought. "That didn't take as long as usual," Emily said.

"Hmph. Well, that might be because we didn't need to discuss your terrible behavior this time."

Emily put on a pout, but she couldn't hold it, and it broke into a grin. She pointed at Jeb's hand. "What's that paper?"

Jeb stuffed the list of books in his pocket. "Never you

mind, Missy."

"And how is the fair Miss Elmore?"

"About the same as when you saw her not a half-a-hour ago, I reckon. Now stop with all them questions, and let's get on home."

At home, Emily started her homework, and Jeb set the supper table. Miss Elmore's problem worried at his mind as he worked. He stopped cold with the plate still in mid-air. He put it down and headed over to hunt for a card he'd placed in the catch-all drawer. Finding it, he went to his rotary phone on the counter and dialed the number in Little Rock. A male voice answered.

"Traditions."

"Is this Mr. Deakins?"

"Yes, Hector Deakins speaking. How may I help you?"

"This be Jeb Compton. Don't know if you recollect, but I were the one sold you my Annie's mirror aways back."

"Why, yes, Mr. Compton. I do indeed remember. In fact, I have it prominently displayed in my shop."

"Well, sir, that's good. That mirror's the reason for the call."

"Are you ready to have it back?"

Jeb hesitated, then made up his mind. "No, sir. I need you to sell it for me if you will."

A brief pause followed. "I see. That's a little unexpected, I must say."

Jeb sighed. "I know. I had planned to take it back when I were in a better place, which I am, but —"

"No need to explain. I'm glad things are better. I mean that. And yes, I can certainly sell it. My customers have salivated over it since I first placed it. I'll make some calls, and I'll bet I can have a nice-sized check on the way in a day or two at most."

"Okay, then. That will be good. I know you be needing your share, and that's fine."

"My share? Oh, you mean my commission. Well, normally I'd take one, but in this case, I'll do it gratis."

"Say what, now?"

"There's no charge for selling it."

"Why would you do that?"

"I like you, Mr. Compton, and we have something in common. Plus, it's that time of the year. Consider it my Christmas present to you."

Jeb fished in his pocket for a handkerchief to wipe the sudden moisture from his eyes. When he thought he could speak without a quaver in his voice, he continued. "Thank you, sir. That's right decent of you. Will you at least take out that twenty you give me for it?"

"Certainly, if that's what you'd like."

Jeb invited Hector to come for a visit, said his goodbyes, then prepared supper. When they were finished eating, he looked across the table at Emily. Weighing his decision, he blew out a breath.

"Emily. I need your help with something, but you can't let on about it to no one."

Emily's eyes lit up. "Count on me, Uncle Jeb."

Three days before the Christmas break, Miss Connie Elmore entered her classroom to find a bulging envelope on her desk. Printed on the front were the words: "For those who have needs. Merry Christmas."

When Emily got home, Jeb asked how things had gone. "It went off real smooth, Uncle Jeb. When Miss Elmore went in the room, I peeked from the door. She looked confused when she saw that envelope, and more so when she opened it to find the money. She read the front again, then her eyes got all sparkly, and she hugged that envelope to her chest. I don't think I've ever seen her look so happy."

Jeb smiled. "Good enough, then. Thanks for filling me in. She didn't see you, did she?" Emily frowned, and Jeb hurried his next words. "No, course she didn't. Sorry, Emily, I should a knowed better."

Emily's frown disappeared, and a smile replaced it. "I'm getting a little hungry."

Jeb laughed. "Well, sir, let me see what I can drum up."

# CHAPTER 33 — SANCTIONED

The screen door slammed against the house in accompaniment with the hound's excited barking. Two forces of nature that were about the same size, but different in dimensions, barreled down the hall and shot into the kitchen. "Uncle Jeb!" Emily yelled.

Startled by the ruckus, Jeb wheeled around. A half-eaten peanut butter sandwich slipped from his hand and landed on the oak plank floor. Seizing the opportunity, his dog Homer pounced on the unexpected bounty and wolfed it down. "What in the Sam Hill?"

Emily, red-faced from exertion and excitement, grinned. "Uncle Jeb, you should have seen it! First day back from break, and those kids Miss Elmore wanted to help all came today wearing new clothes: pants, dresses, shoes, jackets. It made my heart swell to see it. We did good, huh?"

"That's nice to hear, Emily. Yes, we done good. You didn't let on to no one, did you?"

"Of course not. I can keep a secret. But you know —"

Jeb cocked his head at her. "I know what, now?"

"Well, I think Miss Elmore might have her suspicions. She's a pretty smart lady."

Jeb relaxed. "I ain't worried. I'm sure she mentioned her concerns to several folk. And we covered our tracks real good."

"I hope so. I know nobody saw me put that envelope on her desk, but it was lucky that I happened to read that message on it."

"What do you mean?"

"Do you remember what you wrote?"

"Sure. It were, 'For them as has needs. Merry Christmas.'"

"That's right, and if Miss Elmore had seen that, she'd have known who it came from."

Jeb's legs felt weak. He pulled out a chair from under the table and sat down heavily. "I didn't even think —"

"It's okay. It was written in pencil, so I quick-like erased part of it and changed the words."

Jeb blew out a breath. "Thank you, Emily. You saved my bacon for sure."

"Consider that payment for all those wonderful books you got me for Christmas. I have a question, though."

"What?"

Emily looked down at the floor. "You won't get mad at me for asking?"

"I'll do my best not to."

"Okay. Would it be such a bad thing if she did know?"

Jeb fought to keep his composure. "Course it would, Emily. She might think I were doing it for her instead of them kids."

"But, wouldn't it be okay if you'd done it for both?"

"That be two questions, Missy, and one's all you get. Now, I'm thinking you best be starting on your homework."

After Emily left and Homer settled under the table for a nap, Jeb sat thinking about her second question. Hearing about those kids reminded him of the hard times he had growing up, so he wanted to help. He believed his Annie would have cottoned to the idea of seeing her mirror going to a good cause. Jeb folded his arms across his chest. "And that were all there were to it," he said aloud.

He leaned his chair back on two legs and stared at the ceiling. Only it wasn't all there was to it. He wanted to do it for Miss Elmore because she cared so much about those students. He could almost see her beaming when they walked into school with brand new clothes.

Jeb sat forward, the chair legs hit the floor, and Homer jumped. "Sorry, Homer, I didn't mean to spook you. Thinking about all this is messing with my head. I sure enough be interested in Miss Elmore. I admit that, but I ain't feeling quite right about it neither. I don't know what to do." Homer listened attentively but gave no response. Jeb sighed. "How about you and me take a walk down the lane before dinner. What say?"

Jeb went to bed still troubled. He tried to go to sleep, but couldn't clear his mind. Finally, he sat up and flipped on the lamp. Maybe I'll read a bit, he thought.

As he scanned the shelves of his white pine bookcase, his eyes fastened on Annie's favorite book: the *King James Bible.* He reached over, pulled the book out, and propped his back against the headboard. As he opened the book, a folded letter fell out. On it was written "To Jeb" in Annie's neat handwriting. Jeb's hands trembled as he opened the letter and began reading.

*Dear Jeb,*

*If you're opening this Bible, I reckon something is troubling you. I may be wrong (I was maybe once or twice), but I figure it might have to do with a woman. If that's the case — that some woman has caught your attention, I 'spect you're feeling guilty because of me and what we had together. I have one thing to say about that: Don't.*

*Jeb, I know you loved me and were as devoted as a man can be. That means the world, but it's only natural not to want to be alone. You're still young enough, and if you've come across a good woman who'd be willing to put up with you and that ornery hound, I say you should give it a whirl. Whether it works out or not, you have my blessing. I want for you to be happy.*

*All my love,*
*Annie*

Jeb stared at the letter until he noticed teardrops hitting the paper. He swiped at his eyes with his free hand, folded up the letter, and stuck it back where he found it. Annie, he thought, you outdone yourself this time. Thank you, my love.

Jeb woke the next morning feeling more rested and at peace than he had for a good many days. Over breakfast, he caught Emily's eye as she worked her way through her biscuits and gravy.

She cocked her head. "Yes, Uncle Jeb?"

"Emily, I'm picking you up after school today."

"How come? I mean, it's not that I wouldn't rather ride with you than on that noisy, bumpy bus."

Jeb smiled. "So, you prefer that noisy, bumpy truck of mine, eh?"

Emily didn't reply right away. Land sakes, he thought, have I finally stumped her on something? When she spoke, she said, "I'm just curious."

"Well, I need to be stopping by to see Miss Elmore for a small piece, and I thought I'd kill me two birds."

There had been a time when Jeb's phraseology would have left Emily scratching her head, but she'd since grown accustomed to his manner of speaking.

"What are you going to see her about?" Emily gasped, realizing what she had asked. She had been dressed down for treading in sensitive areas of Jeb's life.

"Well, I thought I might see if she's interested in going out with me."

Emily's face lit up. "Really? You mean it?"

"If you recollect, I told you I'd let you know how things stood once I got it sorted out. So, that's what I'm doing."

"That's wonderful! It makes me so happy, Uncle Jeb."

Jeb held his hands up, palms facing Emily. "Now, don't go getting all fired up, Missy. I ain't even asked her yet. She might tell me to take a hike."

"Oh, no. She'd never do that. Not to someone like you."

"Well, maybe. Anyways, finish up your food and go get ready for school."

Jeb drove to school that afternoon, his heart thumping. He met Emily as she came out, told her to wait in the truck, and braced himself to enter the building.

Before she turned to leave, she grabbed Jeb's hand. "Good luck, Uncle Jeb."

"Thank you, Emily. Now be off with you."

As Emily skipped to the truck, Jeb headed for Miss Elmore's room. He sucked in his breath, squared his shoulders, and knocked on the door.

"Come in."

Jeb entered to see Miss Elmore sitting at her desk, grading papers.

"Mr. Compton, I wasn't expecting to see you today. What can I do for you?"

"Well, I had me a question I were wanting to ask you."

"Certainly. Do you want to take a seat?"

Jeb stood there, not knowing what to do with his hands. Finally, he shoved them in his pockets. "No —. I —. This won't take but a minute."

Miss Elmore tilted her head and looked at him. "Okay, then."

"Well, I were wondering —"

A little later, Jeb opened the door of his truck and slid behind the wheel. He put the key in the ignition but didn't turn it. Instead, he sat there, staring out the window. He could feel Emily's eyes on him.

Her voice was timid. "Uncle Jeb?" she asked. When he didn't answer, she said, "Uncle Jeb, what happened?"

"She turned me down."

Emily's face flushed, her eyes narrowed, and her jaw clenched. Before he could blink, she threw open the truck door, jumped out, and ran toward the school. By the time he got out, she had disappeared from sight. He slumped back against the truck and put his hand on his head. Ten minutes passed. Emily came out of the school and stomped up to the truck.

"Emily, what —"

"She wasn't there. I searched, but the janitor said she'd gone home."

"And what —"

Emily stamped her foot. "How could she?"

Jeb flinched. "Emily, calm down."

Tears cascaded down Emily's cheeks. She threw her arms around Jeb's waist, burying her face in his stomach. "Uncle Jeb, I'm so sorry."

Jeb placed his hand on her head and smoothed her hair. "Emily, don't be upset. It will be all right. I been through rougher than this."

"But —"

"Listen. Let's just head on home. We'll talk about this later."

She looked up. "Promise?"

"I promise."

# CHAPTER 34 — DISCOVERY

Despite the late afternoon temperature still cracking ninety, Jeb's mind felt frozen. He didn't remember driving home, parking the truck, letting Emily out, or getting out himself. Now he sat slumped in his porch chair, elbows on the armrests and fingers massaging his temples. He was trying to make sense of what happened. All those lonely days after Annie died, he thought. All the guilt over thinking about another woman.

"Uncle Jeb?" He lowered his hands and looked dully at his niece's face. Homer stood beside her, and both looked concerned. "Uncle Jeb, are you okay?"

"I will be, Emily. Just trying to sort things out in my head."

Emily nodded. "Do you want to talk about it?"

Jeb roused himself from his lethargy. "Maybe, but first I

want to know what you was thinking, running after Miss Elmore like that. What would you have did if she'd still been there?"

"I'm sorry, Uncle Jeb. I was just so angry. I couldn't believe she turned you down. You! And I wanted to make her see how wrong that was." Emily's shoulders trembled, and the tears started. "I'm so sorry."

Jeb held out his arms, and Emily rushed into them. As he soothed the sobbing child, he thought about what to say. "Emily, I think I seen why you did it, and it were good of you to want to stand up for me, but you know it were not the best way to go about it." After a few seconds, he said, "Say, are you thirsty? I could sure use me a glass of lemonade."

Emily stood up, wiping away her tears. "I'll go get us some."

Lemonade in hand and bottom in her chair, Emily looked at Jeb. She chewed on her lower lip for a moment, "Did she tell you why?"

"Right to it, eh? Well, maybe that's for the best. She did not. I don't know if she just don't care for me or if it be something else. She just looked sad and said it were not possible."

"And I'm guessing you don't want me asking her about it tomorrow?"

"Lord, no! You need to stay out of it"

Emily looked unhappy. "Okay, Uncle Jeb." After taking a deep breath, she said, "Uncle Jeb?"

"Yes?"

"If I were to check around some —"

Jeb's eyebrows lowered. "Emily."

"Nothing that would get back to Miss Elmore."

"Emily! That be enough. You need to keep your nose out of this."

"If you say so, but —"

Jeb's face darkened. "But what?"

Emily held up a hand to forestall an outburst. "If I do happen to hear anything, not because I asked, mind you, would you want me to tell you?"

Jeb considered. "Well, I 'spose. It do bother me not knowing." He pointed a forefinger at Emily. "As long as you don't go involving yourself."

Emily looked the soul of innocence as she drew a quick X over her heart with her right index finger. "I promise."

The daily routine at the Compton place resumed: Jeb applied fertilizer to the soybeans, and they thrived. He and Homer did a little hunting and fishing, the hound aiding the first and complicating the second. Emily went to school, then, when her homework was done, she and Homer explored the forty acres before dinner. They took excursions in the truck on the weekends, went to the Dixie Diner once in a while (where she and Sally Lowrey became fast friends), and drank lemonade on the porch while discussing her latest readings. Miss Connie Elmore made no appearance in the daily conversation. Until one day —

Jeb pulled out his pocket watch and flipped it open. Four o'clock. It was about time for Emily to be getting dropped off by the school bus. He flipped the cover of the watch shut, returned it to its lodging, and walked to the front door. He looked toward the lane and saw Emily and Homer tearing down it. They arrived at the house and promptly collapsed on the porch, Emily on her back and Homer on his belly.

Jeb shook his head. "Why is you two hitting a dead run in this heat? Emily, I thought you, at least, had more sense."

Gasping for breath, sweat beading her face, Emily sat up. She tried to speak but couldn't get the words out.

"Never mind," Jeb said. "Just stay still, and I'll get you some water."

He returned shortly with a glass for Emily and a bowl for Homer. "Now don't be gulping it."

Emily followed instructions, and Homer ignored them. When both sprinters had cooled down, Emily said, "Uncle Jeb, I finally heard something!"

"You did, eh? About what, exactly?"

"About Miss Elmore, of course. About why she might have turned you down."

Jeb stood there, dumbstruck. He opened his mouth a few times, but no words came out.

"Uncle Jeb, are you okay? You look like one of those goldfish at the county fair."

Jeb ran his hand through his hair. "I'm okay, Emily. You just took me by surprise."

"Well, do you want to know?"

Jeb hesitated. "To tell the truth, I ain't sure. I mean, I do, but —"

"You're afraid you won't like what you hear?"

"Something like that, I reckon."

Emily grinned. "Well, if you're not sure, I guess I can go start on my homework."

"You got a touch of the ornery in you for sure. Okay, then, let me hear it."

"Well, I saw Sally Lowrey pull up in the parking lot while I waited for my bus to come up in line, and —"

"Leave off a minute. What were Sally doing at school?"

"I didn't ask. I just went over to talk with her for a few minutes. Anyhow —"

"You didn't ask her about Miss Elmore, did you?"

Emily stuck her nose in the air. "I didn't. I promised I wouldn't, remember?"

"Okay, then. Sorry. Go ahead."

"Well, we were talking, and we saw Miss Elmore leaving the building and heading for her car. Sally said, 'That's a real shame about Connie. She's such a good person.' I guess I looked curious because she proceeded to fill me in."

Jeb nodded and braced himself.

Emily took note, and her voice quieted. "It seems her husband didn't treat her right. I think the word Sally used was 'abusive.' That's bad, right?"

Jeb's eyes flashed. "Yes, it's bad."

"Anyway, Sally said Miss Elmore finally had enough and ended it, but —" Emily seemed to be concentrating. "Sally said it like this: 'It left a bad taste in Connie's mouth and soured her on relationships.' I'm thinking that's why Miss Elmore turned you down."

Jeb walked to his chair and sat down with a grunt. He let the conversation sink in for a minute, then looked at his worried niece and smiled. "Thank you, Emily. You done good."

"What are you going to do, Uncle Jeb?"

"Well, after I sit here a mite longer, I think I'll see about getting you and Homer some supper."

"I mean about Miss Elmore."

Jeb sat with his big hands clasped. "Don't seem like there be much I can do. I wondered about why she turned me down, and now I know. Don't figure she's gonna change her mind, and I need to respect that."

Emily got red in the face. "But you're so nice! I've never seen you treat anybody badly. "

"Well, I surely try to be a good man, but I'm unlikely to convince her of that, I 'spect."

Emily looked about to explode. "But Uncle Jeb!"

"Emily, I know you want the best for me, but just leave it be."

Emily stamped her foot. "So you're just going to let her go?"

"Emily, these is adult problems that is hard to explain. Let me say it like this. How can you let somebody go when they was never yours to start with?"

"But —"

"That be enough, Missy. We done talking."

"I didn't figure you to quit a fight before you even threw a punch. I'll bet Emerson wouldn't have."

Having thrown that kidney shot, Emily ran off the porch with Homer in pursuit. Jeb leaned back in his chair and ran his hands through his hair. "Annie, why ain't things ever simple?" He stood up and walked in the direction Emily and Homer went.

## CHAPTER 35 — FINAL ATTEMPT

In Hurlin, the mercury nudged ninety, and the humidity level lagged not far behind, yet a distinct chill descended on the Compton household. After their altercation of the previous day, Emily acted sullen, Jeb felt glum, and Homer, well, being a hound, nothing much fazed him for long.

Propped up in bed the following night, Jeb sought to divert himself from thoughts of the Miss Connie Elmore situation by reading one of his favorite authors, Thomas Paine. Unfortunately, the first passage he turned to read, "The real man smiles in trouble, gathers strength from distress, and grows brave by reflection."

Annoyed, he tossed the book on his bedside table. I'll try me some T.S. Eliot, he thought. He opened the book and read, "Only those who will risk going too far can possibly find out how far one can go." That book swiftly joined the first.

One more time, he thought. He picked out a book by Winston Churchill, opened it, and read, "Never give up on something that you can't go a day without thinking about."

Jeb closed the book, placed it on top of the others, and leaned back against the oak headboard. He looked up at the ceiling in the general direction of heaven. Annie, he thought, I think someone's trying to tell me something. Still looking upward, he mulled things over. Nodding his head once, he got out of bed, pulled on his trousers, and went down the hall to his niece's room. He knocked on the door. "Emily, is you awake?"

A sleepy voice answered. "Come in." Jeb opened the door to see Emily sitting up in bed. Her red curls ranged in all directions, and she wore a Snoopy and Woodstock t-shirt. She knuckled the sleep from her green eyes. "What is it, Uncle Jeb?"

Jeb sat on the end of her bed. "Sorry if I woke you. I were thinking, Emily, and I've come to a decision."

"About what?"

He hesitated a moment, then plunged ahead. "About Miss Elmore."

She said nothing but seemed to wait expectantly.

Jeb's ears grew red, and his voice held a wobble. "I ain't ready to quit yet. One more try be in order."

Emily, still tangled in the covers, nonetheless managed to reach him with a huge hug. "You are talking about Miss Elmore, aren't you?"

The next day seemed to stretch forever. Jeb waited till Emily arrived home, then got in his old Ford truck and drove to the school. He waited while a returning bus went by, then walked to the main doors. Passing through them, he turned down the hall to the open door of Miss Elmore's room. He peered in and saw her sitting at her desk, grading papers. He watched for a moment, then entered.

She looked up, her eyes widening. "Mr. Compton. What are you doing here? I mean, I didn't expect to see you."

"Sorry about that," Jeb said and smiled. "But we got some unfinished business."

"We do? About me going out with you? I thought you understood that I can't do that."

Jeb pulled out a student chair and sat down. "I understand that's what you done told me. What I ain't understanding is the why."

Miss Elmore blinked and looked down. "I'd rather not go into it. Let's just say I haven't had the easiest time where men are concerned."

Jeb spoke so softly, Miss Elmore had to strain to hear him. "Been my experience that we've all been scraped by the gravel road of life."

"Excuse me?"

Jeb spoke again in a louder voice. "We all have past troubles of some sort or other. Mine was in thinking I were being unfaithful to my wife's memory."

"And yet somehow you managed to work around that?"

"I did, with a spot of help. It weren't easy, even after that, but I finally screwed up enough courage to ask you out."

"And I turned you down."

"Yes, ma'am, you did, and I'm admitting it hit me pretty hard."

Miss Elmore leveled her gaze. "Yet here you are. Are you telling me you couldn't take no for an answer?"

"I had to give it another try because I think you're worth it."

Miss Elmore blushed. "But nothing's changed, Mr. Compton. I like you, I do, but I'm sorry. I'm afraid the answer is still the same."

"You sure about that?"

"I'm afraid so."

Jeb stood up and blew out a breath. "Well, then, I done all I can. I won't bother you no more."

When he got home, he saw Emily and Homer waiting on the porch. He slowly got out of the truck and trudged over.

Emily couldn't contain herself. "Uncle Jeb, what did she say?"

"She didn't change her mind."

"What are you going to do?"

Jeb shook his head. "Nothing. I tried again, but I guess it weren't enough. I weren't enough. If that's the case, then it's time to pack it away and move on."

Tears came to Emily's eyes, but she didn't protest. Jeb headed to the kitchen to fix supper.

Jeb sat in his porch chair reading while Homer snoozed beside him. Homer's head abruptly lifted and swiveled toward the lane. A moment or two later, Jeb heard the sound of a vehicle driving in their direction. A blue Rambler American 220 pulled into sight. He judged it to be a 1964 model. The Rambler came to the end of the lane and parked, but no one got out. Jeb looked down at his hound. "You expecting company, Homer?" Homer sneezed. "Me neither. I wonder who it be."

Another minute passed, and the car door opened. Miss Connie Elmore got out. Homer took off in a dead sprint before Jeb could grab his collar. The hound shot over to Miss Elmore and stopped cold in front of her. Miss Elmore spoke to the hound, but Jeb — coming as fast as he could — couldn't hear what she'd said. By the time he got close, she had knelt down and was rubbing Homer's belly. The big hound squirmed around on his back, looking like he'd died and gone to heaven.

Jeb stood there panting, a look of wonder in his eyes. He waited till he'd caught his breath enough to speak. "That do beat all. I ain't seen Homer act like that since my Annie were alive."

Miss Elmore gave the belly one final rub and stood. "Quite a dog you've got there."

Jeb laughed. "He's something, all right. Every time I think I got him figured out, he turns things on their head." Jeb ran his fingers through his hair. "I'm sorry. Where's my manners? Would you be wanting to come up and set on the porch?"

"That would be nice."

They settled in on the porch chairs. Homer lay by Miss Elmore's side, gazing up at her.

Jeb looked at Miss Elmore. "Could I get you a lemonade?"

"Thanks, but not right now. And call me Connie."

Jeb cleared his throat. "Connie," he said, and the name sounded like the start of a familiar song. "I were right surprised when I seen you drive up. I thought, well, you know, after yesterday and all."

"Well, I admit I didn't expect to come here today, but a couple of visitors changed my mind."

"Say what, now?"

"Right after school, Emily came up to talk to me. She told me about how you took her in after her mother died. She said you and Homer, is it?"

Jeb nodded.

"She said you and Homer made her feel like she had a family again when she thought she'd lost everything. And —"

Jeb's head cocked to the side. "And?"

"And she told me about you getting the money to help those children at Christmas."

Jeb frowned. "She did, eh? And after she done promised me she wouldn't." He shook his head. "That girl."

"Don't be mad at her. She did it to advocate for you. She did it because she loves you."

Jeb sighed. "I know. Tell the truth, I'm surprised she held it in as long as she did."

Connie smiled. "Me, too."

"You said a couple of visitors. Who be the other?"

"Well, Sally Lowrey looked me up during lunch. She told me about that incident at the Dixie Diner and what you did for her when that bully was causing trouble. Do you know you're her hero?"

Jeb looked at his feet. "That weren't no big thing."

"It was to her, and I agree."

Jeb shook his head. "Them two. They must have cooked this up together. When I seen Emily on the phone this morning, I thought nothing of it. Now, I reckon I know who she were talking to."

"You have a fan club, Mr. Compton. Anyway, after Emily left to catch the bus, I sat there thinking."

Jeb could feel his heart pounding.

Connie looked down at her hands clasped together in her lap. "I had a bad experience, and it led me to doubt myself and others, but —"

"But?"

"But I think I'd very much like to have a chance to get to know you better. If you're still willing, that is."

Jeb smiled. "Yes, ma'am. I'm willing."

Behind the kitchen window, a quickly muffled cheer erupted.

# THE END

# ACKNOWLEDGMENTS

These folks are responsible for helping me get this book in your hands or on your tablet: Anita Paddock, teacher, mentor, and author. She helped me find my voice and kept me on the path. Marla Cantrell, teacher, writer, and editor. She taught me about resolution and pointed me to the goal post. Sherilyn Walton, fellow high school teacher, friend, and devout reader. Judy Harrington, writer, friend, and cheerleader. The members of the Miller Writers Group, who gave me a reason to keep writing. The Beta readers, who read the pre-published book. Rachel Snider, author and formatter, who helped bring the book to fruition. Kim Bice, photographer, who provided a knock-out cover design. Ruth Wilwers, my long-suffering wife, who survived the insanity. And last – but not least – every hound I've ever known.

If I've unintentionally omitted anyone, my apologies.

Made in the USA
Middletown, DE
24 January 2021